Wayland

Wayland

A Novel

Rita Sims Quillen

Iris Press
Oak Ridge, Tennessee

Cover Photo: Copyright © 1982 by Ron Flanary
Restored C&O steam locomotive 2716 (leased to Southern Railway at the time) blasts out of the north end of Natural Tunnel near Glenita, VA.

Book Design: Robert B. Cumming, Jr.

Library of Congress Cataloging-in-Publication Data

Names: Quillen, Rita Sims, 1954- author.
Title: Wayland : a novel / Rita Sims Quillen.
Description: Oak Ridge, Tennessee : Iris Press, [2019] | Summary: "Wayland is the story of a perfect life interrupted by a chance encounter with pure evil. Eva and Andrew Nettles are a couple who found each other in the unlikeliest of circumstances and married in mid-life, now living a blissful country life with their adopted daughter— until one day a hobo happens by. Buddy Newman cannot believe his good fortune: this family has everything he needs, including the most beautiful little girl he's ever seen or dreamed of. Newman sets his plan in motion to charm and deceive the family and possess the object of his desires. Can they see through his elaborate deceit in time to save their daughter?" —Provided by publisher.
Identifiers: LCCN 2019023857 | ISBN 9781604542547 (paperback)
Subjects: GSAFD: Suspense fiction. | Mystery fiction.
Classification: LCC PS3617.U5356 W39 2019 | DDC 813/.6—dc23
LC record available at https://lccn.loc.gov/2019023857

The poetry and prose quoted by the character Buddy Newman in *Wayland* are all in the public domain. I gratefully acknowledge the following sources for the works in their entirety.

Keats, John. "Bright Star, Would I Were Stedfast As Thou Art." The Poetry Foundation. www.poetryfoundation.org/poems/44468/bright-star-would-i-were-stedfast-as-thou-art.

_____. "Endymion, Book I, [A thing of beauty is a joy forever]. Academy of American Poets. www.poets.org/poetsorg/poem/endymion-book-i-thing-beauty-joy-ever.

_____. "Selected Love Letters to Fanny Brawne." Academy of American Poets. 14 Sept 2009. https://poets.org/text/selected-love-letters-fanny-brawne.

Kipling, Rudyard. "If—." The Poetry Foundation. www.poetryfoundation.org/poems/46473/if---.

Tennyson, Alfred Lord. "Will Waterproof's Lyrical Monologue." American Literature. www.americanliterature.com/author/alfred-lord-tennyson/poem/will-waterproofs-lyrical-monologue.

Twain, Mark. *The Adventures of Huckleberry Finn. The Norton Anthology of American Literature.* Nina Baym, et. al. Editors. Shorter Fourth Edition. New York, Norton, 1995, pp. 1202-1386.

No writer is an island, and so I must thank some people who contributed to this book. I am grateful to the invaluable resource provided by Studs Terkel in his book *Hard Times: An Illustrated Oral History of the Great Depression* and Richard Wormser in his book *Hoboes: Wandering in America, 1870-1940.* Their research and excellent writing provided the information and context I needed to create this world of the 1930s. Deep gratitude goes to amazing poet and writer Jim Minick for his thoughtful feedback on the manuscript, as well as the kind blurbs and words of encouragement from him, Ron Rash, Amy Greene, and Mark Powell. All of my love and thanks to my husband Mac for his constant support and encouragement. My dear friend Linda Parsons provided not only her excellent editorial advice but emotional support and nurturing, as well. Finally, my deepest thanks to Iris Press—Robert and Beto Cumming continue to provide wonderful opportunities for readers and writers to connect, and associate editor Cathy Kodra continues to be every writer's best friend with her outstanding copyediting and developmental suggestions.

I have never met any really wicked person before.
I feel rather frightened.
I am so afraid he will look just like everyone else.

—Oscar Wilde, *The Importance of Being Earnest*

I

When Buddy Newman walked into the dusty little southwestern Virginia town of Gate City, he made sure he had his road face on, a menacing and mysterious dead-eyed stare that would help him survive in the encampment of hobos and tramps down along the creek not far from the train yard. Once he moved out of the camp and settled on a plan of action, chose his patsies or hatched a new scam, he would change himself from the inside out, taking on whatever face he needed, changing even his speech, his gait, his ways of moving his hands. He was as malleable as the clay banks in the hills above his old homeplace. When a man is hollow inside, he can fill himself up with anything he needs, get bigger or smaller, stay fluid or form a solid wall.

Buddy had only been in town a couple of days, but he already had a pretty good idea of the lay of the land as far as his world was concerned. The town had a surprisingly large encampment, what was known in the hobo world as "the jungle," probably somewhere between fifteen and twenty-five people every night, just at the edge of town, right off the main street. They had names like T-Bone, Chicken, Guzzle, and Pip. Almost every town of any size that had railroad access had an encampment of some kind, a desolate, depressing swath of ugliness with blankets thrown over tree limbs making little pathetic tents. Sometimes crates that had carried produce would be taken apart and nailed into a little box the size of a small chicken coop with boards or pieces of rusted tin for a roof. In Gate City, the hobos stayed beside a narrow creek that ran along the lower street. It was a shady place and far enough from any street or house that there wasn't too much complaint unless a disturbance or some vandalism or thieving occurred.

Buddy's real name was Dexter Deel, and he left home from Bluefield, West Virginia, four years before. Holding onto that name seemed like a bad idea, under the circumstances, and besides, even the other railroad bums with no secrets told him right off that nobody used their real name out here. Too much law-breaking to be done, they said. So he chose the name Buddy Newman—because he wanted to always remember to be everybody's buddy, and because he was going to be a new man and make a new life. He was proud of his cleverness.

Buddy liked to ride the blinds—the little platform on the front of some of the cars—but it was unpleasant. You could eat enough soot, gravel, and dust to kill you, but at least you weren't hiding away in a bunch of stinking livestock or waiting to get caught and beat up by some mean railroad thug.

He rode into Gate City on a long coal train, jumping off one of the back car's blinds, just a few hundred yards from the train engine's halt in the station. He always did that; he didn't want to be close enough to the engine for anyone to see him at the station. It was much better to walk into town with no one having any idea how you got there and no railroad bulls bashing you with their clubs or calling the local sheriff.

He started walking at nine months, his momma had told him in between her drunken stupors, so a life comprised mainly of just walking, walking miles and miles a day, many days, or running to catch a train car, suited him just fine. He might have stayed in Bluefield, except the only sane, caring people he knew—his grandparents on his mother's side—had died a couple of months apart, while his mother had conveniently gone off with one of her gap-toothed, mouth-breathing boyfriends and left Dexter to handle all that messy stuff at the end. His father Abraham was long gone, thank God. Mr. Deel's only talent had been cruelty. Dexter's worst memory of childhood was his father punishing him for something he didn't do by hanging the family dog from a tree by a chain and making Dexter stand and watch him swat it with a bat, a hideous yelp coming with every pass until finally it was quiet.

When his grandmother followed her husband to the family plot, Dexter saw to it that they were buried proper with the sale of the few animals they still had left. He kept his grandfather's pocket watch, knife, hunting rifle, and an old pistol. He gave the keys to the old house to their neighbor, Mr. Williams, with instructions that after one year, if his mother didn't return to claim it, Mr. Williams could sell the place, keep ten percent of whatever it brought, and mail the rest to Buddy in care of the Salvation Army Mission there in Gate City.

The town had been a good choice for the mail-drop location because it had good train service from everywhere, and he had a friend there. One of the Salvation Army "sisters," Molly Kate O'Donnell, was a friend he'd grown up with. He always joked with her about being a "doughnut Christian" because he only showed up at Missions and churches for sweets, strong coffee, and conversation. They both had a good laugh about it; she knew there was probably no hope of changing him, but she would never stop trying.

Buddy had been riding trains and working odd jobs for these four long years that felt like forever—a very long life for a hobo. Many died trying to hop on or off a moving train, or from malnourishment or disease, or they were killed by somebody for stealing or being on railroad property. It was a dangerous life. If anyone tried to get on the train in a safe manner while it was stopped, he was much more likely to be caught by the railroad bulls. If he was lucky, they'd just rough him up and throw him off the train. Often, however, people got hurt bad or killed if the bulls recognized them as repeats.

Buddy was good at hopping trains; it's one of the reasons he'd lived so long. It took practice to learn the exact moment to break out of hiding and run alongside, waiting for the chosen car to catch up so he could grab hold of something big enough to offer a good grip. A man had to have the strength to swing free of the earth and pull himself up there. It was painful; the strain on his wrists felt as if it would break his hands clean off, and his ribs felt as though they were separating. He'd heard every story anyone could imagine.

One guy named Slim Jim got his head cut off because he stood in the doorway of a boxcar, and when the train pulled out, it caught him off guard and knocked him down. He couldn't get to his feet quick enough to avoid the heavy door's rush. A bunch of shifting freight mashed another man they called Tater. It fell on him while he slept as the train rounded a curve up the Blue Ridge Mountains. Somebody told Buddy that he was broken and mashed so bad, they like to never got him scraped up off the floor.

In the Gate City jungle, there were tramps and hobos, and probably quite a few were like Buddy and moved between both worlds, meaning sometimes they would work if they felt like it and it was fairly easy, but if they didn't find an easy path, they'd just steal or run a scam. Because of the little group of nuns there, the town attracted lots of his kind. The nuns had money and big hearts: what more could these struggling souls ask for? The camp was full of guys with a sad story to tell. One of them who called himself Chicken Joe claimed to have a dying mother in North Carolina who he was trying to get home to see. Several claimed to have jobs waiting down in Tennessee or Georgia if someone would just see fit to stake them the money to get there. There was a "dummy" pretending he couldn't hear or speak, but Buddy saw through him right away when the man jumped and yelled out at a big clap of thunder.

Buddy laughed and laughed at the man and cussed him and threatened to beat him to death while he slept. The man had disappeared by the next morning.

That wasn't the only problem, though. A gang of tramps hung around, the kind who wouldn't work, what the wandering folks called a "push." It was a mixed gang, some old and some young, and it was a nasty piece of work. A man appropriately named Iron Mike ran the gang with an iron fist. The gang bragged about killing lots of people, mostly railroad bulls and other hobos who crossed them. Iron Mike was the sort of man Buddy Newman hated with a white-hot passion he could feel in his gut, the kind of man who thought he was invincible, better than everybody else. Iron Mike had a young boy named Isaac with him who he protected from the others, and Buddy had seen Mike stroke the boy's hair at the edge of the campfire light. The boy didn't seem to like it much, and Buddy felt sick to his stomach for him. He'd heard about those kinds of gangs. He'd have to see if he could think of a plan to help that boy out.

Getting away from the jungle, and from the stares of the good town folk and the suspicions of the local sheriff and his deputies, seemed like a good idea. Buddy never liked towns or cities. He felt uneasy and exposed. They had too many variables he couldn't control, too many players, too many moving parts.

No, he liked the country better for lots of reasons. That's why he'd headed out toward the back side of Scott County. There were train depots at Fort Blackmore and Dungannon if he needed to leave fast, but what really drew him was the kind of people he knew he'd find there. They'd be good country people, innocent, God-fearing and hardworking, poor enough to have a lot of sympathy for someone like him, but prosperous enough to have resources he could use.

When he crossed Copper Creek and started the long climb over the first big ridge, he immediately felt the rushes of cool air that seemed to come up out of the ground, the sweet smells, the wonderful quiet. He made sure he changed his face. In some of the big cities, he'd made use of more educated and sophisticated people, and he used what he called his Professor face, pretending to be an educated man, a teacher, down on his luck. Here he decided to go for his Country Boy face. He pressed the corners of his lips into a perpetual little smile, a clown face, opened his eyes much wider, made sure to relax the furrows of his brow. He worked on remembering to nod his head slightly every minute or two, like he always agreed with what someone was saying. He loved this character, and it had helped him in many a small town or wayside around the southern states.

He saw a sign on a church that read Wayland Baptist Church; he'd heard a man on the street in Gate City tell another man he lived out in Wayland. "Wayland." Buddy said it out loud to himself and smiled. Wayland would show him the way to what he wanted.

When Eva Nettles cracked the window open to let in the morning air, soft as a spider web on her face, she laughed at the cacophony of birds madly chirping, the hens clucking and putting, the cows bawling for their babies in the field. She was so happy these days, she had trouble sleeping. The green and gold promise of spring was everywhere. The wild mustard set the hills on fire, and the first whippoorwills' sweet calls drifted across the silky evening air for the first time the night before. Life was too exciting, too fun, too promising to waste time in bed! She made sure she was up when the sky still held pink fire, the steam from her first cup rising like the mist from the hills.

Things that she'd given up on ever having were all hers now. Almost everything that had been taken from her had been given back: the baby she lost so many years ago had been replaced by a beautiful, precious little girl named Katie, her brother Ezra's child, whose mother had died of consumption soon after she was born. The first husband she'd lost to fever had been replaced by Andrew Nettles, a military man who'd given up the career he loved to be with her and help her raise Katie.

The dilapidated three-room house of her childhood was replaced by a beautiful whitewashed farmhouse with green shutters, a wide porch, and huge windows where she could sit and draw or paint or quilt in her very own room, overlooking a green rolling carpet of pasture surrounded by trees that gleamed gold in spring and dazzled with ice diamonds in winter. With the Great War finally over and the local economy growing, the uncertainty of poverty had been replaced with a small but growing cattle herd on their own little farm and with Andrew's sawmill. They were both mortgaged, but so far, making the payments was no problem.

This beautiful April morning, the air smelled sweet and warm, the sky was almost purple, and the trees were gold-gilded and shimmering. Her spirits had been lifted by the sunlight and longer days, and the journal that had kept her occupied for the long, long winter evenings, pouring out stories from her childhood and all her worries and fears and secret thoughts, now lay gathering dust on her Bible table. Eva had started out to get some fresh eggs when she heard sounds from the henhouse that she knew weren't the usual. She froze, backed toward the back door, and eased it open to grab the rifle she kept leaned in the corner. Andrew was at the mill, and if this was a local thief or a tramp, she'd have to deal with him herself. She kicked open the door and fixed her daddy's Winchester rifle right between his eyes. Eva's heart pounded. A man with shoulders as big as a hay wagon had a hen tucked under his arm, but he instinctively raised his hands. The chicken squawked and hovered and began to flog him.

The drifter fell to his knees right into the chicken droppings, yelling, "Wait! Wait—don't shoot!" The chicken pecked a bloody spot in the top of his head, and Eva lowered the gun slightly and backed out into the yard.

"You get up and come on up out of there, or I'll shoot you."

The man walked out into the yard with his hands still up.

"I ain't got nothing in my pockets but my skinning knife, ma'am, and I ain't here to hurt you. I'm just really hungry, and I'm out of tobacco. Been walking for a long time." His eyes were intense and piercing, but guarded and exhausted, too.

His voice was gentle and deep. He looked to be someone trying to make a good impression despite his raggedy coat and vest. Eva had dealt with tramps before. Most of them would come right up and knock or come to you in the yard asking if you had any work or any food to share. Andrew had fired a warning shot one night when he'd heard something out in the henhouse, but they had never seen anyone. The next morning a hen was missing. She and Andrew had sympathy for all these poor souls, but couldn't let word get out that the Nettles allowed people to steal from them.

"You could knock on the door, and I'd give you some bread." Eva kept the gun pointed at him. "But you ain't stealing my chickens. Katie! Katie!" She yelled as loud as she could, never taking her eyes off the man.

A little girl with long chestnut hair soon appeared in the screen door. The man reacted as everyone did the first time they saw Katie's shining hair and perfectly shaped face. A solid bead of sweat appeared on his forehead. He stared at them without blinking.

"Bring a biscuit out here to me in a sack." The girl obeyed, but was obviously frightened, never taking her eyes off the man as she backed up to a table by the door.

When Katie returned, Eva laid the biscuit on the stack of feed bags and backed away from the man. "I don't want to shoot anybody, but I'm taking care of what's mine. Katie, get in the house." Eva stepped inside, too, locked the door, and watched out the window. The man stood there a minute, lowered his arms slowly, and then picked up the food Eva had left. He walked quickly out of the yard, wolfing down the biscuit as he went on his way.

Down at the Clinch Sawmill, Andrew was already covered in a fine dust, and the smell and taste of the wood he was cutting filled his nose and mouth. The spray of shavings off the logs filled the sunlit air and sparkled like crystals. The men couldn't talk over the roar of the saw and belts, so they moved in a quiet pattern, each inside his own head and body, focused on the quickly moving wood, repeating the same motions over and over. It was a ballet of muscle and motion that was obvious to Andrew, and he would often stop and smile to himself at the beauty of it all.

Many people in Wayland had rolled their eyes when they first heard that Andrew and Eva were opening a sawmill. "That fancy boy is gonna find out what work is, for sure," someone said. The community was polite to Andrew, but he would always remain an outsider. Eva's willingness to marry the man who had tried to catch her brother Ezra when he went AWOL from Camp Lee and to put him in prison was considered sad and embarrassing for her.

Eva and Andrew were aware that they were the source of gossip and raised eyebrows. It didn't bother Eva at all, but Andrew was different. He had never felt like he belonged anywhere, and Wayland wasn't going to be any different. All his life he'd looked for a group of men to sit with and laugh and tell stories, like his father Jimmy, who never saw a stranger and had more friends than he could name. So far, Andrew hadn't really found them. Eva's brothers were polite and helpful if he asked, but he wasn't someone they would pal around with. The brothers went hunting and fishing together, and only once had they asked Andrew to join in. The men at the sawmill worked for him, so he wasn't a buddy they would pal around with on weekends. There was no getting around that barrier. So it was really no surprise that he reacted like he did when Buddy Newman showed up.

Andrew was so tired when he arrived home that evening that his legs felt as heavy as the logs he'd been sawing. He stripped off his dust-covered, wet clothes and wiped himself down enough to put on his old overalls to go in for supper. They had all just sat down at the table—Eva talking a mile a minute, telling him about the tramp she caught in their henhouse earlier—when they heard a strong knock at the back door. This was unusual because almost everybody who ever came to the back door was family, and they pecked lightly on the door and walked on in. When Andrew rose and opened the door, Eva's mouth flew open. There stood the man she'd caught trying to steal her chicken. He had cleaned up since the morning encounter, face scrubbed clean, his thick, curly dark hair combed straight back.

"That's him!" Eva cried as she shot up out of her chair. "The man that tried to take one of the hens!"

"Ma'am, please." The man squeezed his hat nervously. "Ma'am, I come to apologize." He looked at Andrew. "My name's Buddy Newman, sir. I wondered if I could have a word with you." Andrew didn't look at Eva as he stepped out the door and closed it behind him.

"You gotta a lot of brass, coming back here. My wife told you she'd shoot you if she ever saw you again, and she ain't a woman to make idle threats."

Buddy Newman let a hint of a grin cross his lips. "That's why I waited 'til I knew you'd be here. I figured you for a levelheaded man." He studied the ground a minute and grew serious again. "I'm ashamed of what I become. But I was so tired and hungry. I'm still hungry right now."

Eva opened the door and started to say something, but Andrew gave her a look. She drew her mouth into a straight line that said "All right, fine." She slammed the door shut again.

"Mr. Nettles, your wife done fed me once, even with me trying to steal from you. I'd like to repay you all. If you'll let me, I'll go cut you some firewood—I'm talking oak, not pine—and split and stack it right there." He pointed to the side of the shed. "If you're satisfied it's worth it, maybe you'll see fit to let me have another biscuit or piece of cornbread."

As he listened to Buddy Newman, Andrew kept thinking he knew him from somewhere. He racked his brain trying to remember where, asked Buddy lots of questions. But he had no luck. Then it hit him. His looks were very different from his daddy, but Buddy Newman sort of reminded him of Jimmy Nettles.

Buddy had that same kind of self-confidence and masculinity, those qualities other men admired, but Andrew lacked. He figured Buddy would slap his leg and laugh in the middle of a big story just like Jimmy Nettles would. *I bet Jimmy Nettles would have loved Buddy Newman. They would have been best of pals.* Andrew smiled to himself. He decided to give Buddy a second chance, to try to understand being hungry enough to steal, to be kind and generous to the man with the spirit of his daddy.

"Come to the Clinch Sawmill in the morning, Mr. Newman. We'll try you out for two weeks. If I decide you won't work, I expect you to clear out of here, understood?"

Buddy Newman lit up and said, "Fair enough. Thank you. I'll make you a good man, you'll see. I wasn't always like this."

Buddy thanked and thanked Andrew, shaking his hand twice, telling him he wouldn't be sorry, telling him a big sob story about hurting his leg jumping from the train.

Buddy made a note in his journal as soon as he left the Nettles' home, before he could forget he'd told Andrew it was his right leg. Buddy smiled to himself as he wrote it down.

When he got back out to the main road about a mile from the Nettles' home, he took out a knife he kept in his backpack and drew three straight, slanted lines on a tree. That was a warning to other hobos not to go down that road. Usually, it meant there had been a hostile or violent reaction to some other wandering soul, or maybe there'd been arrests or attacks from the railroad's Pinkertons. In this case, it was a lie, one used anytime Buddy Newman found a new patsy. "Keep going, boys, keep going," he said out loud as he made the mark. "Find your own way."

Katie Teague was a remarkable child. Her dark hair had been streaked by the sun, gleaming like satin when she moved in bright light. Her perfect face featured stunning blue eyes, lashes so thick they didn't look real, and full rosy lips. Her skin, always tan, came courtesy of the Cherokee blood on Eva's maternal grandmother's side of the family. Katie's momma, Alma, was a beauty, too, but everyone agreed Katie surpassed even her. Many women would have gladly traded any financial gains for this wondrous inheritance.

But looks weren't her only special trait. Katie had an amazing mind, too. She told almost no one of her deep thoughts and questions, of the unique turns of phrase and questions that came to her, of the strange feelings of sadness and awareness she often had. She told no one that she often lied to Auntie and Uncle Drew, telling them she was going to visit her best friend Alice when, in truth, she walked off somewhere to be alone. There was a high pasture over on James Baker's farm that she loved, the highest place around that she could reach easily. The breathtaking view encompassed that wide valley all the way over to Moccasin Ridge and up almost to Russell County.

She'd sit there in the almost constant breeze, the wind whirling past her ears in a white roar. She also loved to go to a cool, shady bend in the little branch below the church where the trees created a canopy like walls. She could sit in there and feel as though she was in her room at home; no one could see her.

Katie carefully considered and examined everything she heard or experienced. Comments in church and at school, remarks grownups made, what she read in the stacks of library books she kept in her room—all were filed away to be called up when needed. The things she heard at church puzzled and worried her most of all, especially Judgment Day. It made a cold sweat pop out on her if she thought about it much—the sound of a horn blowing, then the earth splitting open and the dead rising up. She couldn't think about it very often or she would never be able to get anything else done or consider another idea.

One thing was for certain: Katie was different from most kids her age, and she understood this from a very young age. Once, on a blustery and unseasonably cold October Saturday, she insisted on bundling up and going out anyway. No one else was outside. She felt like the last person left on Earth. She stood under a big maple tree in the back yard, and a gust of wind burst through the tree, every leaf and limb twisting into a choir of jubilant voices. She held out her arms and closed her eyes and became part of that sound. She often had the same sensation when a big thunderstorm came through. She loved to run outside and lie flat on the ground, letting the rain splatter her face. Eva got mad at her for doing this and would always make her come inside.

She never told anyone her dreams. She'd heard other people tell their dreams, like something chasing them, or thinking they were at school without their clothes on—that sounded horrible! People dreamed they were flying or in some Alice-in-Wonderland world where things were completely crazy and unreal. She sometimes had dreams like those, but mostly her dreams were something else, something so strange and other-worldly she was afraid to mention them. She dreamed of foreign countries and big cities that looked real, but she had never been any place like them. Sometimes she dreamed as if she were another person in another time, looking out at the world through their eyes.

In one of Katie's recurring dreams, she stood at the foot of the bed of a beautiful woman. Curtains blew in the breeze from an open window to her left. The woman's face was shiny and pale, the hands gripping the bedpost at her feet were tiny, a child's hands. Katie had this dream over and over. After she dreamed it for the fourth or fifth time, it suddenly came to her that maybe the dream was not a dream, but a memory of watching her mother die. But she'd been just a baby when that happened, not even walking yet.

Katie decided she had wanted to stand there at the foot of that bed, even as a baby in someone's arms. Her mind had made it true for her, so she could be there and watch her mother's soul lift and fly out that window on the breeze, feel it leave that beautiful shining face and float overhead.

Katie's head was always so busy, she needed a lot of time alone. School wore her out. Going somewhere to be quiet and alone felt so nice. Her favorite hideaway of all was the tree house that belonged to R.J. and his friends. Not far off the ground, it had been built in a crooked oak on R.J.'s place by his dad for a deer and turkey hunting blind. The hideaway barely measured four feet by six feet. The kids had carried a couple of old milking stools up there, and Katie enjoyed sitting and looking out over the pasture through the small window. Something about being by herself, with no one talking except the leaves and birds and bugs, made her happy and led her to fantastic thoughts.

It was in the tree house that she remembered being in her crib, still a toddler but amazed with watching the sun rising through the rails and the window beyond, and with no cry for anyone to come get her. She had tried to tell Auntie about this one day, but it had just made her aunt laugh and say no one could possibly remember being that little. Katie hushed then and knew she would have to learn to keep a lot of her memory and special knowledge to herself. No one would understand.

Though Eva was still just in her teens years ago when she lost her baby and her husband, she had thought her life was over, too. In fact, she wanted it to be over. No one could imagine what it was like to feel that kind of hurt, to survive a sorrow so deep that her chest hurt. She couldn't breathe, couldn't think, couldn't possibly sleep, except in little fits and starts. The fatigue was so overwhelming a few weeks in that her legs and arms were too heavy to lift, and food felt like cotton stuck in her throat. But then, on top of all that, her daddy had a stroke, and there was no time for grief. Eva had to step up.

She helped her mother care for him from daylight to dark. He was like a baby then, so she tended to him as if he were her own little one, sang him to sleep, bathed and changed his clothes and sheets. This was her life, and it healed her day by day. Then her mother got sick, too. It would have been more than she could bear if she let herself think about it.

But Eva seemed born for trouble. She handled it, did what needed to be done. With help from her siblings and neighbors, she cared for both of them until they could lie side by side up on the hill at Mt. Pleasant Cemetery overlooking the beautiful Moccasin Ridge and the Clinch Mountains. Though she still grieved, a time had finally come when life was good: Ezra was out of his mess and married to Alma, and they had a beautiful baby girl, Katie, who Eva loved from the first moment she held her. She even dreamed of her almost every night.

When Alma died from tuberculosis only a few months after Katie's birth, once again, Eva found herself with no time to grieve, to question, to work through her frustration or anger at the way life had, once again, been so cruel to her family. Ezra fell apart and even under the best of circumstances would have been ill-prepared to raise a baby. No, this would be Eva's responsibility. People would comfort her and offer sympathy that she was again "stuck" with taking care of other people, but Eva looked at them like they were crazy. Didn't they know this was her second chance? She would probably never have children of her own, but this was the closest thing.

Besides, Eva knew what most people didn't: Ezra had just stopped living after Alma died. He stopped everything—eating, laughing, talking, telling stories, playing his banjo, working—everything. He took to drinking, something he'd never done before. After Eva found him passed out for the second time, she brought him home with her and made him stay. It took a lot of talking, lots of cutting firewood and mending fences, lots of long walks down to the creek, and lots of praying before she got him to see that he had to get his life started back. He straightened himself up and ventured out into the world again, but he had changed. The Ezra that was the life of the party and everybody's friend seemed to be gone.

When Andrew Nettles, the man who had hunted Ezra, left the Army and showed up on Eva's doorstep with a ring and a plan, it was awkward for Ezra, to say the least. But the two men had developed great respect for one another in the years Ezra had been on the run from Andrew and the military. They bonded over the fact that they both had tremendous respect for the military, but at the same time a tremendous exasperation at the complexity and senseless bureaucracy. The two men bonded mostly, however, over their mutual love for Eva, so they had surprisingly little problem talking their way to a mutual understanding and mutual forgiveness of the long ordeal. As far as they were concerned, everything that had happened was the government's fault anyway. The war and the military itself seemed like an illness they'd both recovered from. They shook hands and put it behind them.

It wasn't that simple with all Eva's family, friends, and neighbors. Two of her brothers didn't speak to her for months. It nearly broke Eva's heart; she never dreamed they would hold that kind of grudge, especially after Andrew testified on Ezra's behalf at his court martial. She tried to explain to them that he was just doing his job; the Army couldn't let people walk away with no punishment at all. They had finally come around. The Teagues were a very close family, and they loved and appreciated Eva for who she was and what she'd endured. Andrew was still not their favorite person, however, with his proper ways and talk.

Andrew Nettles grew up on a quiet street in Big Stone Gap in southwest Virginia, not too far from Eva Teague's Scott County home. His father had been a successful businessman, owning a hardware store in town. His mother, Roberta Arnott Nettles, was the only daughter of one of the town's "old money families," people said. In truth, they didn't have much money, but they had property and status and pretensions. Roberta's mother had insisted on dressing for dinner, always wearing a hat whenever she went out, having ladies over for a book club luncheon, all things her mother had told her went on every day in the world outside "these hills."

All the Nettles' neighbors knew that Andrew wasn't from around there and that his family, the Arnott family, had come to Big Stone Gap when almost everyone else had: during the coal mining, railroad-building days in the 1880s. Stories still circulated in the local lore about Roberta's mother, who everyone referred to as "Miz Stella," getting off the train in a beautiful burgundy silk dress and a hat with a big feather, with ten trunks of clothes and household items loaded off on wagons.

Stella was a big-city girl from up North who never completely adjusted to the mud, the gray fortress of hills around her, or the roughness of her Big Stone Gap neighbors. While her husband Jacob worked in the railroad office, she ran their home like a business and raised her children, Roberta and Millie, with one purpose: to persuade them to leave the godforsaken place and make something of themselves. She punished any hint of a mountain accent in their speech, visibly shuddered if they used words like "recollect" for "remember" or "hit" for "it." But to her bitter disappointment, it didn't work. Roberta, her pride and joy, fell in love with a smooth-talking, handsome local boy named Jimmy Nettles and settled into a house right down the street.

Jimmy was one of those mountain men for whom words were currency. He was a storyteller extraordinaire, his talk vivid and imaginative and original. As spellbound by him as everyone else, Roberta's own speech was sprinkled with his imagery and colorful similes. When Roberta told one of her friends to stop "grinnin' like a mule eatin' saw briers," Miz Stella frowned. When Roberta complained that her mother's chicken dinner was as "tough as whit leather"—leather treated with alum or salt—the double insult was too much, and Miz Stella took to her bed with a sick headache for three days.

After Roberta and Jimmy ran off and got married, her mother never completely recovered and never forgave Roberta for her treachery. Even so, the apple doesn't fall far from the tree, and as she aged, Roberta also groomed her children for life outside the hills and hollers, outside this backward place where people's speech was different from anywhere she'd ever been. Nothing superficial, nothing people could acquire or display, could erase what their speech and voice revealed about them. Andrew Nettles wasn't a mountain boy; he was never "of" this place. Eva's brothers and sisters never let her forget it, either.

"He just ain't one of us, Eva. Don't have much in common," Eva's brother John Michael had said. "But long as he's good to you and you want him around, it's fine with me. I'll be nice to him." He'd kissed her on top of the head and never raised the subject again. Eva wished Andrew could be one of the boys, go hunting and fishing with them, or just visit and target shoot, all the things her brothers loved to do. But it wasn't meant to be.

Ezra had a different attitude. Ezra didn't serve in the military long, but he knew Andrew's standing up at that court martial and telling his superiors they should give Ezra a break took guts and character, and Andrew paid a price with some of his fellow soldiers for helping one who'd refused to go through the same hell they'd been through.

So Ezra owed Andrew, as far as he was concerned, even if Andrew had ruined his life for two years. He had been eager to help his new brother-in-law set up a sawmill, something he knew a little about. He began to find his way back to himself, playing his banjo and telling stories again, smiling and laughing and playing pranks. He would even hold Katie and rock and sing to her sometimes, but he held back, Eva noticed. His face sometimes turned sad and pale when he looked at his baby girl.

One day he stepped through the back door while Eva was feeding Katie her dinner and started dancing a little jig and singing a silly rhyme to her, and the baby had laughed out loud for the first time, a big belly laugh. Thrilled, Eva clapped her hands and laughed. Ezra laughed, too, but then his eyes filled with tears.

Eva reached out and took his hand. "I know. I know it's hard. You miss her so."

"I can't, Eva." Ezra stopped and wiped his eyes and face. "I can't do it. The only way I can go on and live and not go jump off a cliff or drink myself to death is to stay away from Katie. It hurts me so bad I can't breathe." He pulled Eva close and hugged her. "You'll never know how much I love you, and thank you, Eva. You're a wonderful mother for her. Alma is so happy and comforted, I know." He stepped away and didn't look back at Katie as he hurried out the door. It wasn't long after that he started coming by a little less often. By the next year, he was gone, off to work at another man's sawmill for what he thought would only be six months or so. Life had other plans for him, though, changing the story, shifting the landscape right out from under him.

These days, Andrew Nettles was a man sick to death with worry, but no one would ever know it by looking at him. He hid things well, always calm and deliberate, very polite, meticulous in his appearance and his speech, disciplined by years in the military. Andrew could have had a rattlesnake in his pocket and never let on. He was as calm as pond water.

Just a few years earlier, Andrew had been on top of the world. How could someone's life change so dramatically in just a few years? After the war and his time of chasing the men who went AWOL, his plan of staying in the military and moving on up the ranks had been altered forever by his time here in Scott County, chasing Eva's brother Ezra, one of the most cunning and frustrating deserters.

Andrew Nettles had come to Eva's little country house to try to convince her to help him bring her brother in. What he found was this tiny, adorable, gallant lady who looked like a child with her freckles and sun-bleached hair, caring for an old man who was like a baby. Eva had only a mewing cat and some chickens and a cow to keep her company. Her chin jutted out in defiance of this government man who showed up at the door. Andrew felt ashamed and questioned his zeal to pursue these men. As he watched her care tenderly for her father while also risking life and limb to help her brother evade capture, Andrew discovered he had found his true calling in life: to love and protect Eva Teague. It wasn't a conscious decision; something about her just got to him like nothing else ever had. At the first opportunity, he left his military career and its ambitions behind and came home to southwest Virginia.

When his mother died and left him the house in downtown Big Stone Gap, along with a little money, Andrew proposed a week later. He never questioned why Ezra left his daughter Katie with them. He knew it was best for everybody, especially Eva. If anybody had taken that child from her, it was hard to tell what would have happened. He and Eva married one Sunday morning after the regular service in the little church Eva attended. Afterward, the couple signed a note at the bank to buy equipment to open a sawmill.

With his friend Mac, who he'd met during the search for Ezra, Andrew had the perfect partner for his business. Mac was one of those men who could do anything—mechanical minded and smart. Andrew could always count on Mac to figure out how to do anything needed. They'd been a great team. During the boom years right after the war, the Clinch Sawmill had kept expanding and buying equipment, hiring more men and wagons, but now Andrew was worried about how he would pay for them all, though he hadn't told Eva anything yet.

Things had been going great until the last year or so. But now people didn't seem to have money for anything. Prices for crops had gone from sky high to the lowest in years, and no one made enough money from the crops to pay for the seed and other expenses to put new crops in the ground. He'd never seen anything like it. His business had really slowed. He'd always hired helpers by the job. There were plenty of folks willing to work for a while and then go back to their farm or somebody else's farm. He'd kept things small enough that he could get by, but that was about all he could do.

He never told Eva any of this. He lived by her smile, the sound of her humming as she quilted or painted or worked in the kitchen. Her life had been so much harder than his, so sad, so uncertain. He couldn't bear to disappoint her, and to fail her was unthinkable.

They were like two planets in different orbits, connected by a force so powerful it could never be broken, but different in almost every way, somehow disconnected at the same time. Had Andrew known Eva had secretly saved a lot of money she planned to use to buy more land, a mountain would have been lifted from his shoulders. He would be able to pay his note off at the bank and own the mill free and clear. Had Eva even suspected what trouble the mill was in, she would have gone straight to the bank, paid off the note, and started saving for the land all over again. But these two were Mars and Venus, spinning on, hurtling through stardust and blackness, suspended by the dark energy that bound everything together.

Buddy Newman was so alert and excited, he, too, had trouble sleeping. The Nettles were like finding a goldmine. They had a beautiful home, a business, money, horses, and, most of all, Katie. He had already fixed his sights on Andrew and chuckled about his innocence, his sad-eyed loneliness and self-pity. A poor excuse for a man, and had he not had so much that Buddy wanted, he and Andrew would have never had more than one conversation. But with this family's potential prize, Buddy was more than willing to put up with whatever and whoever he had to.

Wayland itself was also perfect. He wasn't much to care about such things, but even he had to stop sometimes in his wanderings and look at the stunning views. There were several places in the community where he felt as if he were standing on a cloud, the ground falling away sharply, opening up to a valley of rolling green and ribbons of water where he could see for miles.

And the people were fascinating. Many of them were members of families that had been in this area for well over one hundred years. Their names were familiar to everyone, and they were often related by either blood or marriage. What pleased Buddy the most were all the crazy characters he met. There was a man who still wore his war uniform on a regular basis and walked the roads daily. A lady named Betty Sue went to every revival and "got saved," each time telling a new story about some awful thing she'd supposedly done. A family everybody knew had children born of incest. Another woman claimed to be a witch. It was all fascinating to Buddy, but even more interesting to him was the fact that people seemed to take it all in stride. Nobody bothered anybody much or got upset with these various characters. They actually seemed to enjoy the strangeness.

This live-and-let-live attitude was perfect for Buddy. He could keep his focus on the prize he wanted. He figured out quickly that he'd have to concentrate on Andrew and Katie—Eva was one of those hard-muscled, tiny spitfire women that Buddy hated. Fiery, high-tempered, and independent, she thought she could do without the help of any man. Andrew would be easy; Buddy had him pretty much from the start. He would have to tread cautiously with Katie, but of course, that was part of the thrill. What would it take to reel her in, have her trust and care for him, pity him, feel guilty for not making him happy? Buddy giggled and shivered with pleasure at the thought of how and when he might first touch that silky hair and soft, warm skin.

Buddy's quiet takeover of the Nettles family happened so fast and natural that nobody thought anything of it. At first, Buddy was just that guy staying in the little office at Andrew's sawmill. Andrew let him put a cot in there, and with a little pot-bellied stove he could use to heat a pot of coffee, Buddy was tickled to death to have such luxury. He thanked Andrew over and over, promised he wouldn't be sorry, said he'd keep firewood cut for the office and his family's house. "I'll be the best man you ever saw," he told his new boss.

Buddy asked Andrew many questions about a lot of things. He'd ask about his family and childhood, he'd ask what kinds of guns were best for hunting. He peppered him with questions about the equipment at the mill and so on. Andrew loved it. He enjoyed having someone care about his opinions. Though he was a little reluctant to talk about his family and childhood, Buddy's seemingly sincere interest gradually drew him out.

Buddy pretended to have a daddy like Andrew's. He told tales about times he'd disappointed his daddy, times he and his dad had gotten in trouble with his mom for their shared mischief. Buddy laughed to himself about it later and wrote notes in a little brown notebook, which he reviewed from time to time to make sure he didn't get his facts tangled up later.

As Buddy and Andrew grew closer, Andrew started inviting him to come eat dinner with them on a fairly regular basis. Buddy's table manners weren't the best; he ate like a starved pup, slurping and sometimes chewing food with his mouth open. But he provided entertaining company. The family saw his talents right away, as he made them beautiful gifts. He found cherry limbs that had fallen out in the pasture between the house and the sawmill, and one day, he showed up for supper with the most beautiful polished box. It had a black forged lock and hinges and a rabbit-fur lining. An etching of a bear walking through some trees decorated the top.

Andrew stared open-mouthed. "Where did you get this?"

"Huh. I made it, Andrew. Been working on it since I got here. Got the wood in your field and the hinges from an old door I found down in the dump pile at the creek. It's big enough to hold a pistol, or you could keep knives in it." He turned to look at Eva and Katie. "And I ain't leavin' you out. I'm going to make you all boxes, too, when I get time."

Eva could tell Andrew was touched and tickled to death with his gift.

More than his constant presents and thoughtful, helpful deeds, Buddy's company and gift for gab endeared him to everyone in the house. His account of the world of hobos and tramps was fascinating to all of them. He could talk for hours about what his first days on the road were like, what dangers he faced, how scared and tense he was as he tried to figure out how to survive. Katie took a special interest in the "hobo sign language" he tried to explain.

"Show me." She ran and found her writing pad and a pencil. "Teach me how to make some of the signs. I bet R.J. and Little Jim have no idea about it. They will love it!"

"Well, let's see. If you show up in a new place and you're sick, look for a small "r" carved somewhere. That means they'll try to care for you. That's a good thing. But if you see three lines in a row, leaning right, like this," and Buddy drew the marks in the air, "move on. It means they ain't friendly to tramps and hobos. They might throw you in jail or worse."

Eva's life had been small, in the house or at most a few miles here or there to visit, go to a revival, or to the little town of Gate City for supplies. But Buddy had seen the whole country! He told about riding logs down the river to Knoxville, about crossing over the mountains to Asheville with its rich ladies and mansions. He told stories of his family that held them spellbound.

"My father was a strange man," one of his tales began, and Buddy leaned back and crossed his legs, lighting his pipe again while Eva poured them all another coffee. "My momma died young. I stood at the foot of her bed and watched her die just a-squallin'. I remember my Aunt June trying to pry me loose, but I wouldn't budge."

"That must have been awful," Katie said, looking up from the puzzle she was working, her eyes dark with sadness and sympathy. "You're just like me."

Eva, Andrew, and Buddy all turned to look at her.

"I lost my momma when I was a baby, too. Except I don't remember it. I wish I did."

Buddy nodded and thought what a streak of unforeseen good fortune this was, this deep connection he already had with Katie without even trying.

"Yeah, that's a hard lick, girlie, to lose your momma. It *was* awful. Daddy went plumb crazy after that. Became this religious nut. On Sundays, we couldn't say a word all day, and if he caught us doing anything but reading the Bible or praying or walking in the woods to ponder God's glory, he'd beat us with his razor strop. He chopped my baby sister's hair off like a boy's so she wouldn't be vain and took down all the mirrors." Buddy finally grinned a little at Andrew. "I didn't know I's so ugly until almost two years later when I got to see myself in the big window down at one of the stores in Bluefield." Andrew chuckled, and Buddy threw his head back and laughed too loud and too long, as if he wanted to blow all those memories out into the cloudy dark.

Andrew began inviting him to join them most evenings. "He ain't got nobody, Eva. No woman to cook for him the way Mac does. And you got to admit, he's entertaining."

Buddy would almost always bring little gifts of some kind. He gathered irises and peonies of all colors for Eva and arranged them into a bouquet with cattails from down along the river. He brought Katie an Indian arrowhead he found and a drawing of what he called an "Indian princess." For Andrew, he brought a deer antler polished and sharpened to be used as a knife handle, and he sawed another one into little pieces that could be used as decoration for a coat or a man's hatband.

Eva was a little concerned. Yes, he could tell good stories. But it felt weird having someone like him, someone they didn't really know, around all the time, in their house, like he was a member of the family.

It didn't take Eva long to realize Buddy was no ordinary drifter. The few others she'd ever had any interaction with were often drunks or didn't seem right in the head. Most of them couldn't even read or write. But Buddy Newman didn't fit the mold. Every week seemed to bring some new and stunning revelation. They knew he had artistic ability, but its depth and diversity continued to be revealed. One evening on the porch, he pulled a coin out of his pocket and handed it to Katie.

"What's this for?" she looked puzzled.

"Look close at it," Buddy said, puffing on his pipe.

Katie looked at the nickel in her hand again and turned it over and over, a grin appearing on her face as she looked back up at him in wonder. "Did you do this?"

Buddy only nodded.

"Momma, look at this." She jumped up and gave the nickel to Eva. The coin had been altered, the normal raised carving of the Capitol in Washington had been turned into a beautiful bird on a dogwood branch. Work so detailed, so tiny.

"How?" Eva said. "How did you do this?"

"I just studied until I found the bird and then chipped away everything that was something else." He let a grin curl his lips. "A watchmaker let me have his little magnifying glass headband and some tools with tiny, sharp points. They call 'em hobo nickels."

Eva had never heard of them before Buddy came along, and she was amazed and fascinated. Buddy pulled several new ones out of his pocket. One had been transformed into a scary skull with earrings and a scarf, like a pirate. Another one featured a beautiful mermaid. One had been crafted into a bunch of strange interlocking, intricate geometric shapes. Eva shook her head in disbelief.

He reached into his pocket and pulled out a tiny cloth pouch. "I use these little tools." Inside the pouch were a sharp nail and a thin chisel with a wooden handle, along with his watchmaker's glass.

"Can you make one just for me?" Katie peered over his shoulder.

Buddy turned and smiled the biggest smile at her. "Sure, girlie. What do you want on it?"

Katie wrinkled up her nose for a moment and then smiled. "A beautiful doll, like Mrs. Blair had in the store at Christmastime."

"Well, I'll have to go down there and look at one, but I'll do my best. Anything for our sweet girl, right, Andrew?"

They first became aware of Buddy's knowledge of poetry after supper one cool spring evening. They made a cozy fire and enjoyed fried apple pies for dessert. Eva cleared the dishes while Andrew and Buddy sipped on coffee and Katie read. The house had fallen quiet except for a soft clucking from a hen out back and the rustling of the tree limbs in the yard. Buddy lit his pipe and puffed little rings, making a soft "p" sound, and Katie looked up at him and the sound and smiled. She had told him she liked the smell of pipe tobacco because it reminded her of her uncle, Eva's oldest brother Edward, who Katie had called Papaw as a baby, and that pleased Buddy immensely. Not many women appreciated tobacco that way.

He puffed on the pipe a few more times and then began to speak softly, without looking up at anyone. "A thing of beauty is a joy forever: / Its loveliness increases; it will never / Pass into nothingness; but still will keep / A bower quiet for us, and a sleep / Full of sweet dreams, and health, and quiet breathing. / Therefore, on every morrow, are we wreathing / A flowery band to bind us to the earth, / Spite of despondence, of the inhuman dearth / Of noble natures, of the gloomy days, / Of all the unhealthy and o'er-darkened ways / Made for our searching: yes, in spite of all, / Some shape of beauty moves away the pall."

Katie shut her book and looked at him with her head cocked to one side, and then toward her mother, who stared at him slightly open-mouthed. He stopped then, staring far beyond the floorboards, beyond this little house in the hills.

"Well, my goodness, Mr. Newman, that was quite lovely. Did you write that?" Eva remembered her mother's love of poetry and wished she were here.

"No!" Buddy looked irritated. "That's John Keats, for heaven's sake."

"Oh, yes." Eva felt embarrassed and irritated, something she'd experienced several times in his presence. For some reason, he often made her feel like some uneducated bumpkin. "I remember now. We studied him in school. So you're a poetry lover, Mr. Newman."

"I'm a mind lover, Miz Nettles. I'm a life lover. I've been a lot of places, seen a lot of things, endured a lot. I learned to recite poetry as a way to stay sane, keep my wits, and keep myself alive."

He turned the pipe around and pointed the stem at Katie. "You should learn poems, young lady. Expand your mind. Grow a thick skin. The world is a hard place."

7

Eva's Journal

Winter 1930

I do not have my brother Ezra's gift with words, but as the long, dark evenings are making me walk the floor in boredom, haunted with dark thoughts, I have decided I would follow my brother's footsteps and keep my journal going. Ezra and I were very lucky to get to go to school and have a wonderful teacher who made us want to learn. My momma and daddy were so proud of our "book learning" and our good penmanship. Daddy would show people our writing, grinning from ear to ear! Ezra says writing is all that has saved him, that it's only on the page where he can truly be himself, that no one else really knows him except his book and pencil.

He can write the most clever, most interesting things. He was always the story-teller, the joke teller. Even when we were little kids, all the older ones would pick at him and get him to play his banjo, tell tales. They would laugh and punch him in the shoulder and tell him, "You're just like your grandpa. You're Rupert made over." And it was a compliment.

I was invisible, partly because I was a girl, and girls don't get invited to sit on the porch with the men and learn to tell tales. They're stuck in the kitchen cleaning up the mess after Sunday dinner, and besides, if I'd come out there on the porch and started telling big funny stories and talking in funny voices the way Ezra would do, or started playing banjo or fiddle music, that would have been very frowned on, and Granny would've give me a stern talking-to. Besides, that just wasn't me. I've never had a lot to say. I like to read and draw, all by myself, preferably outside.

Right now, I am stopping to look at the pencil in my hand, because I am fighting so hard to keep it from doing a drawing of a bird I saw yesterday. It feels strange to make the curves of the letters and not of bone, skin, leaf, or something real and tangible. This feels dangerous somehow, but I am determined. During the years when I got to go to school, I would make posters for the schoolroom walls for each holiday. The proudest day of my life was the day I won the "God Bless America" contest the school sponsored. I was so nervous and excited to walk into the Shoemaker College halls and see the posters children from all over the county had submitted all down the hallway walls.

When I got to the auditorium and saw all the people, I felt like I would throw up, but then I saw my poster up on an easel at the front of the room! They had me come up front and accept my prize: a blue ribbon and a silver dollar! They even took my picture with the principal and Mr. Richmond, the hardware store owner in town who had sponsored the contest. The picture appeared in the local paper that week, and Momma cut out the picture and taped it up near the kitchen window. The poster is still hanging in Katie's bedroom, and the newspaper cutting was carefully folded into the big family Bible.

Almost Spring

The dreams would always start in winter, too, and that's the main reason to dread it. When the last leaves fall off in fall, I can't even describe how I feel. Because it won't be but a few weeks usually until the restless dreams and not being able to sleep come. A lot of times, all I remember is David's face floating by, laughing and sweating like he just came in from the field, then he's ash-faced and thin, lying in bed as the diphtheria took him. It was strange how his death is all my dreams bring me, almost never happy images of his courting, love-making, working in the garden together. But at least my baby we lost is always fat and blonde and perfect, sitting on my lap, the smooth roundness of her little legs and toes clear and vivid as if she were alive. Still, I wake up so exhausted and sad I can barely move. But I learnt a long time ago: the winter was made for handwork—my quilting and painting saved my life at least a dozen times. I love to make quilts. I know all of the common patterns: the Double Wedding Ring, the Flower Basket, the Log Cabin, the Trip Around the World. The Double Wedding Ring that Momma made me when I was 14 and packed away for my wedding day is still a favorite. The first quilt I made myself was the Log Cabin. It pulled me through that first long winter after I married while David worked at the sawmill.

And that next winter, when I waited for my baby, too sick to eat, feet too swollen to walk, a Crazy Quilt was all I could muster. It wound up unfinished, uneven with jagged edges like the rest of life, after our Sue Ella was born early and sick. When we buried her under the shade of the poplar grove, I wrapped her in that quilt.

David tiptoed around me that spring, said little, but watched always with those piercing black eyes of his, blaming me somehow, I thought at the time. Of course,

I know now that wasn't so, that was my grief and the Devil after me. To fight the swirling sick thoughts in my head, I quilted right on through the summer that year, even as the weather grew sticky hot. I made a Drunkard's Path, a blinding blue and pink tangle of color and shape like the one that won at the Wise County Fair. The spinning wheel, the butter churn, the flower and vegetable garden were all left untouched that year, and the house grew silent, more dusty, more stale every day. I remember days at a time that were a blur except for the needle and thread and squares of cloth. I'd quilt for days without end, stopping only to cook and eat a little, my hair stringing down like a horse's tail, my clothes stained and smelling of sweat. I wouldn't bathe sometimes until David made me.

I don't like to talk about what happened next. I really ain't never told anybody that when the first chill of winter came in the air that next fall, I shut the door and went to bed. For the first few days, I sat in bed and quilted some when I was awake. I quit talking, quit cooking, quit cleaning. Really, it sounds strange to write it, but I sort of forgot how. My mind didn't work right. David stayed home with me, so he lost his sawmill job. By November, the store wouldn't give any more credit and we had nothing much left except some potatoes and apples in the cellar. There was no flour or cornmeal to make bread, and David paced the house with a gaunt, hunted look.

I still cringe at the thought of David begging me to get up and help him, to help myself. I'm so ashamed that I was so weak. I think of all the things people go through, how lots of women I know have lost babies and kept going. It took the shock of David just about losing his mind to finally make me wake up and come back to myself.

Keeping Diaries

I am so glad I started this. Ezra was absolutely right. Writing things down is amazing. You feel a peace, like something is finished. You let go of so much on paper. It's a great place to leave everything bad, like sorrow and worry and anger. And it's a wonderful place to leave good stuff, too. You can write all day about what you love, things you've seen, the people who hold your heart. I'm sleeping better since I started writing things down. In fact, I told Katie she ought to try it and I even bought a little notebook I found at the dimestore in Gate City. I don't know if she will or not. She's already starting to wonder about things I say, wonder if I really know what I'm talking about. She'll be a sassy teenager before you know it.

More about Writing

I am amazed. Since I started writing in this book, I've been flooded with memories of all kinds. It's so strange that you don't think about certain things unless you start writing, or at least I don't. I don't understand why writing about all this family stuff brought my mother back so strong that I got teary-eyed and had to lay the pen down the other day.

It seems that what I remember most is her cooking and canning. I was overcome with it. I was thinking about all those apple blossoms outside, about how they're a promise of something delicious in the fall: apple butter. My mother had my great-grandmother's brass kettle. Every fall, she would haul that out, call all the family in, and start peeling apples. We'd work for two days, peeling and cutting those apples into little quarter moons.

It would take a day to stir off a big pot over the hot fire outside, the smell of wood smoke and cinnamon burned into our clothes and hair. It was a special thing to be old enough to help make apple butter. You had to be responsible. You had to know how to use the big wooden paddle so that the apple butter never stuck to the bottom of the pan, how to keep the fire at just the right height under the pot, how to put wood in without burning your fingers. The most important job of all was using the big silver dipper to put the apple butter through the funnel into the big wide-mouth jars, all lined up on a wooden bench, like people waiting at the altar rail for communion. Katie is old enough to fill them up this year, and I can't wait.

Momma loved making apple butter better than anybody I ever saw. She said apple butter was "spring come to fall." And she would always laugh and say, "This will eat way better than a snowball this winter." She loved canning in general. She canned everything she could. We had rows of green beans, October beans, corn, tomatoes, apples, pears, pickles, beets, sausage, and tenderloin—row after row of jars in the dirt cellar under the house. In the years when the garden was plentiful, she'd wind up giving stuff away. And she always canned all the extra she could and gave it to her grown children. Oh, how we take mother's love for granted! How we think nothing of it, like she has to do it, or we deserve it! We aren't smart enough to see it's just like Grace—from the same impulse, the same miracle.

Spring Cleaning

Today I got started sweeping winter out of the house. In winter it's no use wearing yourself to a frazzle with cleaning. You keep the mud tracks and wet leaves out of the house and that's about it. But when it's warm and you can throw open the windows and scrub every inch with a bucket and soapy brush, wash your curtains and drag out the cobwebs, it is the best feeling ever. The world made new.

Katie was big enough to help me this year, and she worked good. We had a chance to talk and I was shocked at how grown up she is getting. She wanted to ask about her momma—asked me all kinds of questions like what was her favorite color? Her favorite food? I did my best to remember. I think Katie's just now getting big enough to miss her, and I feel so sad for her.

She don't mention much about Ezra—she thinks a lot more on the dead parent than the living one. It puzzles me some, but who can say how I would have reacted if I'd never known my momma. Mothers and daughters are twin hearts. Anything that separates them, whether it's death, circumstance, disease, or disagreement, leads to a pain and emptiness that nothing will fill. I wish I knew for sure that I could fill that hole in Katie's life well enough to make her whole, but I don't.

8

Eva had set up in this same exact spot in the side yard at least half a dozen times. She brought out her big drawing paper and lots of pencils and a comfortable chair that she placed off to the side of the house. She dearly loved the weeping willow tree behind the house. It was the reason she'd always dreamed of living in the house. Facing toward the tree, fence, and storage shed, she closed her eyes and tried to imagine the drawing with some chickens there beside a much younger Katie playing with one of her dolls.

When her late sister-in-law, Alma Newton, and Alma's father Sam had lived there, she and Eva sat out under that tree and laughed and gossiped and drank coffee on several beautiful Sunday afternoons. The tree was a symbol to Eva. It meant peace, security, happiness, family—everything good. She didn't understand why it made her feel that way, but it did, and she always thought if she could just live in that house, she'd have all those things.

She kept wanting to draw the tree so people would feel the same thing. She'd set up out here and tried and tried, drawn and erased a thousand lines, it seemed. Today a warm breeze tickled her face with her hair, and a thrush in the willow sang at the top of his lungs. The sun warmed her skin, and she left her eyes closed until she could see every line of the drawing in her mind. It was as clear as yesterday.

Engrossed in the drawing, she didn't hear anything until Buddy Newman spoke right behind her.

"That's right good, but, of course, the shading needs work. That's what always needs work."

Eva jumped and nearly dropped the pad. "You like to scared the life out of me. I didn't even hear you." She looked at the drawing again. "Shading. You mean the shadows, the depths, right?" She wanted Buddy Newman to understand that she did know a thing or two about art.

"Yes ma'am. It's what makes the difference between great and just common. But don't let me bother you. You go ahead. Just about anybody would want to draw that tree. It's something, isn't it?"

In a few minutes, Katie came running out of the house to find the cat and ran over to see Eva's work. Buddy beamed at her and reached into his pocket. Between his thumb and middle finger, he held today's gift for her—another perfect apple.

"You must think I'm a horse, Buddy. You always bring me an apple."

Buddy threw his head back and laughed loud and long. "Oh, girlie! You're something. Yes, you're a little filly."

Katie giggled, too, and Eva thought how Buddy was sort of like a grandpa to Katie, something she'd never had. Katie crunched into the apple and peeped over Eva's shoulder.

"Very pretty, Auntie. I wish I could do that." Katie looked up at the tree, then back at the drawing.

Eva stopped drawing to look at Katie, at her lashes so heavy she looked like one of those made-up city women, flawless skin like a porcelain doll. Katie rested her hands on her thighs and bent down to study the drawing more closely. Buddy Newman leaned up against the house and smiled as Eva brushed Katie's silky chestnut hair out of her eyes.

"You two are a picture. Yes sir, quite a picture." He came toward them, and Eva saw something in his hands. He held out the most beautiful little redbird sitting on a dogwood branch, all carved from one piece of wood, the bird so perfect you expected it to lift its head and fly. He handed it to Katie, and then pulled another one out of his pocket, this one a wren, and gave it to Eva.

"These are amazing," Eva said, and Katie nodded in agreement. "I seen lots of whittlin' in my life, but never seen it look—I mean never saw it look—like it's going to just lift its head and sing or speak. Did you teach yourself?"

Newman stared at Katie, a little half smile on his face, and never took his eyes off her as he answered, "Yep. Can't nobody teach you stuff like that. You're either born with it or you ain't." He puffed on his pipe and repeated, "You're either born with it or you ain't."

He turned and walked away slowly, leaving Eva feeling uneasy, as he often did. *I reckon that was directed at me. He's got more talent than me, and he knows it.*

Eva looked at the drawing for a long time and tried again, working a little longer on some of the lines, drawing and erasing, drawing and erasing. After a while, she gave up and stared at the little bird in her lap.

She soon put up her supplies and started supper. She forgot about the tree drawing, too busy with other things.

One morning about a week later, Eva rose to fix her coffee and found a drawing on her kitchen table. It was the willow tree with her sitting under it, only prettier, the sketchpad in her lap with the same miniature drawing on it. Katie stood beside her, a beautiful angel, stunning with wings made of the same cloth as the flour-sack dress she'd worn that day. It was an amazing drawing, far superior to anything Eva had ever drawn or would ever be capable of. The initials BN appeared at the bottom right.

Eva sat down with her coffee and said her morning prayers over it, marveling, almost weepy with the joy and the sadness that such a talent existed, but not for her.

9

Eva would have had a very different reaction to the stunning drawing of her and Katie under the Magic Tree, as she called it privately, had she known the door it opened inside Buddy Newman's brain. He'd fought long and hard to stay away from young girls, tried to stay busy so it wouldn't happen again. But no man like him could have missed the pull of a child like Katie. She was the most beautiful creature he'd ever seen, more beautiful than the dappled foal he'd never forgotten from childhood, more beautiful than any woman he'd ever been with, more beautiful than those movie women he'd seen at the picture show.

He'd fought this urge all his life. He couldn't remember a time when he didn't notice women, always imagine he could see through their clothes. It took him a long time to admit to himself that he liked little girls best. Even in high school, he'd paid way more attention to his friends' little sisters than he did them, but people thought nothing of it at first, just thought he liked children. Some people even suggested he might grow up to be a schoolmaster.

That all changed when the little Barnes girl told her family on him, about him asking her to let him see down her panties. They told his daddy, and it had led to a nearly fatal beating. The old man had broken a rib, Buddy was pretty sure, as well as his nose, and it was a long, long time before it healed. For a while, he swore off girls altogether, but eventually, nature won out.

His first girlfriend was petite and boyish looking; she could have passed for twelve rather than her age of sixteen. But within the year they courted, she grew up in every way, and Buddy lost interest in her. By then he was old enough to know he faced a real challenge; where could he find women who looked like little girls?

Meeting Katie and drawing her under the willow had opened the cave door where he hid his longing and flooded his sleep like nothing ever before. He dreamed of her every night: sometimes she ran in slow motion, looking like she did every day in her little flowery shift. But other times she swam down at the river, naked and shimmering in the water. A few times he dreamed her warm and soft on top of him and woke himself groaning in desire.

The series of drawings began then, and over time they grew increasingly erotic. He finally worked up to one with her legs spread wide like he'd etched on many of the coins he'd carried, and as he stared at it, he pleasured himself one night until he went to sleep, the drawing lying on his chest when he woke with a start a few hours later. He had jumped up and realized then that he needed to stop.

If I was to sleep to morning and one of the others or Andrew hisself came in and found me like this, he'd kill me. He'd tie a rock to my neck and throw me in the river, or have Mac do it.

Buddy gathered all the drawings except one, one of the prettier ones of Katie standing in the water as if rising from her bath or her birth as a mermaid of the river, beautiful and perfect, eating the apple just like Eve. He kept that one hidden, as his token of love for her, in his satchel. He burned the rest, watching the sparks fly up into the evening sky, the seeds of his own destruction safely burned away.

Mr. Newman

I don't know what to make of Andrew and Mr. Newman. Andrew is normally a person who has no use for people who break the law or even stretch the bounds of what's decent and Christian. I can't understand for the life of me why he would basically just take in a stranger, and a hobo, no less, who tried to steal one of our chickens! It doesn't add up.

But they do seem to be getting on good, and Andrew says he's a real hard worker down at the mill, so I guess that helps. I puzzle over the way Andrew has just about made Mr. Newman one of the family. He eats supper with us nearly every night, and he and Andrew will sit and talk almost until bedtime, out on the porch. Sometimes their voices drop down to a soft murmur that's part of the beautiful quietness of night time. Other times, they get so tickled I get tickled at them, without even knowing what was so funny. They laugh loud and long, Mr. Newman with that weird funny giggle of his, and Andrew with that rare, head back, openmouthed holler of a laugh that I rarely hear from him. Mr. Newman has a ton of funny stories. Some of them are not something they want me and Katie to hear, so they make sure to shoo us off to do something else.

Even having said all that, it doesn't change the fact that I don't trust him and wish he wasn't here so much. I know it may be wrong of me—that's judging someone. But he makes me uneasy. I don't know why exactly. It's not just because he tried to steal my chicken. Many a hobo or tramp has stole something to eat. I can't say I wouldn't do the same thing if I got hungry enough.

No, it's something else. There's a look that crosses his face sometimes that I can't explain. It's generally directed at me or Katie. I can't put my finger on what the look is, what triggers it, or what it means exactly. The closest I can come to describing it is the look you might see on the face of a proper, well-dressed lady who just stepped in a cow patty.

Gossips and Hypocrites

I'm so mad I could spit nails and build a dog house. Went down to the store to get a few things and some of the older ladies were gathered up in a knot talking to Mrs. Blair. They spoke but got quiet when I walked in.

I decided to make the first move, so I stopped and chatted. One of them, that old Mrs. Jones that lives over on the main road, says, "Do you folks ever hear from your brother Ezra, Eva? If you do, please tell him me and Mr. Joe say hello." She always called her husband Mr. Joe, even to her children. She's crazy as a bat. Pardon me, but she don't give a dried-apple damn about him or Katie, she's just wanting to be nosy. I glared at her for a minute to make her squirm, which she did, and then I told her, "He ain't able to come back here. He's a very sick man. He's got another family now to tend to as best he can. But don't you worry, Katie's more than fine, and Ezra sends her money."

I bid them a good day, got my groceries, and walked out without looking back. That'll give them something to gossip about. I didn't really lie: he did send her money a few times, but that had been a couple of years earlier, before he had so many more children.

Ezra finally remarried a few years after Alma died. He met Mary Anne when he went down to North Carolina to run a sawmill for a man who was injured and couldn't work. Andrew had told Ezra about the accident. A log had rolled off a pile and crushed his foot, and the fellow was going to be laid up a long time. His nephew was one of Andrew's Army buddies, knew he ran a sawmill, and sent Andrew a letter, knowing one of his Army brothers would come through for him one way or another in a crisis. Ezra was happy to help out and eager for a change of scenery. He had no idea it would change his life like it did.

He met a woman down there, married, and had a baby on the way before we knew a thing about it. He ended up staying and running that sawmill for over a year. The man's foot finally healed. Ezra came home, but not all the way back to Scott County. Mary Anne, his new wife, had people over in northeast Tennessee, and she wanted to be near them to help with her children and care for her parents. He was in a hard place. By this time, Katie was three and called me and Andrew Mommy and Daddy. Ezra sent me a picture of him and Mary Anne, and I showed it to her, but she wasn't interested. Katie didn't even recognize him.

I didn't know what to do. I would never come between anyone and their children. But I had the strong feeling Ezra was okay with how things were. He finally showed up to introduce us to his new wife and baby—and by this time she was expecting again!—and so I had to ask him, when I got a minute alone with him. It floored me when he said I must keep Katie. Said it wouldn't be treating her right, tearing her away from the only momma she'd ever known. Said he would always love her and let her know that she was his, and tell her all about her mother when she was old enough. Promised he'd help raise her as far as buying things she needed.

God help me and forgive me if I was wrong, but I cried and hugged him and thanked him. I think he did the right thing. I do. Love doesn't just come from whose blood is in your veins. Feeling safe and cared for, neither. I determined that day that Katie would never want for anything my heart and my hands could give her.

Katie has had a rough life in many ways: I can't imagine losing my momma before I got to know her. Just can't imagine. But God did give her a little prize in return, for all the mess life has brought her: she is truly the most beautiful thing I ever seen, even prettier than her mother Alma, which nobody would think possible. Such beauty had to lead to something good. It just had to.

Monday

I declare, you can't ever know when you get up in the morning what's going to come your way that day. I was over at Blair's store and talking to Gladys Stallard. She told me about finding hobo signs, which I'd never heard of until Buddy told us about them. She knew because she volunteers some at the Mission in Gate City. She said the hobos told her about it, and then she went walking on a pretty morning and saw some of it herself.

She said those signs showed someone wants other hobos to go away. There were signs scratched in trees—two overlapping circles that stood for handcuffs. This warned that hobos were subject to arrest just for being here and in the camps. At the intersections of several roads, a mark warned of a barking dog or a man with a gun. Who would be spreading these fearsome warnings? And why would they do that? I've never heard of any violence towards hobos other than Pinkertons putting them off the train or getting them arrested. I honestly can't think of anybody who would bother a hobo at all unless the hobo was bothering him or his animals.

My Treasure

There had been enough money coming for a good while, not so much lately, but back when the mill first started up, Andrew hadn't noticed a little unaccounted for here and there, hadn't wondered what I did with money for the projects I always seemed to have lying around—quilts and drawings and other little artistic things to sell. My big secret is I saved up almost $1000 to buy a piece of land. I can't hardly wait to see the look on his face when I tell him about the money. I've almost busted a few times from keeping the secret, especially if he gets down and worried. One more big check from the sawmill, and I'll tell him. We'll go see Uncle Bert and buy that piece of creek bottomland he'd always promised me. Oh, how I wish Momma could see it, that we are only a few months away from being what she would consider rich! Who could have ever dreamed I could have so much when Momma and Daddy and all my brothers and sisters lived in such desperation all those years before?

I don't talk about this to anyone, don't want people to think I'm pitying myself, and I sure don't want to be ungrateful. Momma would kill me for that. But I have to say that growing up, I got really tired of being poor sometimes. Most people weren't in much better shape than us, but there were a few that had nice clothes, year-round shoes, had baby dolls and puzzles at Christmas. Oh, how I coveted those dolls! Unless you've been without yourself, you can't imagine how hard it is to keep your mind clear and your heart soft, to not grow bitter and jealous.

I have so much more now, I can't believe it, but the challenge still hasn't gone away. Now I have to try to keep my mind clear and my heart soft and away from pride, from forgetfulness of what it's like to live without.

Buddy & Mac

I went down to the mill today to take Andrew his dinner because he told me they had a big job and was a little behind. I went ahead and took some eggs and a biscuit for Buddy, too, because I knew Andrew would fuss about it later if I didn't. Buddy didn't even say thank you, of course, just started wolfing it down. I made Andrew sit down a minute and eat and drink some water. He looked exhausted, and his face was red as a pepper.

While we were talking I noticed something. I could be wrong. Andrew says I imagine stuff, read too much into little things, "borrow trouble" as my granny used to call it, by imagining bad things that haven't even happened yet. But I noticed for the first time that Mac don't like Buddy at all. It's plain as day. They don't speak or even look at each other. And Mac's got this stone face on him I never seen before today. Andrew has never said a word to me about it, and that's kind of important. With only four or five workers here all day, at most, the fact that two of them, one being the boss along with Andrew, can't stand each other is pretty important. What in the world could have happened? Or is it just a personality thing? They are really different. Mac is very quiet, hardly says a word, and he's a family man and a churchgoer. He probably sees Buddy as mouthy. And I bet Buddy is jealous of him, being the boss and all. I'll have to ask Andrew about it, if I can ever catch a few minutes when Buddy isn't around.

Ezra Writes

I got a letter from Ezra today, and he put two dollars in for Katie. I miss him so much, miss his laugh and telling his big tales, miss him playing music. I so wish Katie could learn music. If we had the money, I would have loved to send her to Mrs. Derting to take piano lessons. I just think that's such a beautiful instrument. I love to watch Mrs. Derting's hands when she plays at church or at a wedding. Her hands are magic. They move so quickly to just the right key, and the way she lifts them, with her wrists sort of limp, the fingers seeming to not want to leave the keys. It's lovely. I know Ezra would have loved for Katie to learn, too. I know Ezra would have loved a lot of things that haven't happened.

His letter said he was getting more crippled and more in pain all the time, said he had to walk on crutches now if he went any distance at all. His poor wife has young'uns to tend to (they've had two more) and him, too. I don't see how she does it. It seems he was just cursed in this world, can't get any good luck, can't have anything come easy, things that most of us have and take for granted.

Katie Growing Up

Sometimes I look at Katie and can't believe what I see. Just in the last year or so, she is starting to look so grown up, starting to show a little woman shape about her. I just smile and shake my head watching her play with her kitten. It seems like yesterday she was climbing around and getting into everything, and I couldn't take my eyes off her. Now, she's my little helper—wants to help do the chores and learn to cook. I don't know how we let life go by us like that and not remember it. I don't remember all those days in between her breaking things and now wanting to make things better.

One thing I've started doing just because I know Ezra would have done it if he could is to teach her about nature—about birds and animals and the woods. Drew isn't really that much of an outdoorsman or farmer, not like Ezra or my brothers. But I want her to know things like that. We've started going for walks, and I've pointed out the names of trees and wildflowers, birds and bugs.

Every Sunday we walk along the quick, clear little branch on the neighbors' farm and watch for a grouse and we seen it twice, the same one we're sure, who startled us both when he flushed in a flurry of wings. We found a bee tree, and I told her all about the queen bee and how she works and rules everything. One day we saw a blue heron, with those ridiculous legs, lift off the creek near Hale Springs and talked about how nature was full of mysteries like the blue heron—it made no sense that a bird made like that could fly. There's so much to tell her. To know the woods is to know the ways of God, I tell her, the face He shows us. To read the Bible is to know His mind and His will, I said, but it's Creation where He reveals himself, and we best pay attention. I was proud of myself for thinking of it, and she took it all in, I could tell. We've got to take lots more walks. I've almost waited too late. It's almost time for her to get interested in boys and such, and I'll have no luck getting her to try to catch tadpoles or name birds then, I'd suspect.

Mac saw from the start that Buddy didn't like him. When Andrew introduced them, Buddy wasn't friendly at all, just gave Mac the up-and-down look, didn't smile or try to connect. This puzzled Andrew because it was a complete difference from the way Buddy had acted during their first introduction, but of course, that was after Eva had already threatened to kill Buddy for stealing a chicken. Buddy Newman had a lot of ground to make up and wanted to get in Andrew's good graces and perhaps get a job. He had no such motivation to charm Mac. Buddy apparently saw Mac as the enemy: Mac had the job, the position, the status, and most of all, the trust and confidence of Andrew.

Mac initially tried to be friendly and make small talk, but it was clear that, for some reason, this new hired man had already made up his mind he wasn't going to like Mac.

Mac did as Andrew asked and started showing Buddy around the sawmill and explaining how things worked. Buddy wouldn't even look at Mac when he talked.

"Let me introduce you to the Dockery brothers. They haul for us a lot."

Jacob and Joshua Dockery were fraternal twins. You never saw one without the other. They were big as pine trees. They both offered a hand when Mac told them Buddy's name and said he'd be working at the mill some. But Buddy kept his hands in his pockets and just nodded and grunted at them. The brothers looked at each other as though reading each other's mind about how to handle such rudeness.

"I guess you're one o' them what lives down in Gate City in what they call the "jungle," ain't ya? I don't see how you stand that," Joshua said. Jacob folded his arms and studied Newman with a hard stare. "I heard they had to round up every one of 'em and put 'em in jail last week when they had a robbery at the hardware store."

Buddy Newman's eyes narrowed a little and his face flushed, but the men standing around the circle didn't seem to notice in the bright glare of the midday sun.

"The ones I know don't never do such as that. Might steal a bite to eat." He glanced at them and then looked down in shame, remembering how he'd met the Nettles in the first place. "Don't talk unless you've been a mile in another man's shoes."

"Oh, that ain't never gonna happen," Jacob giggled. "Ain't never stickin' my feet in no stinkin' hobo's shoes!" He slapped Joshua on the back, and they laughed together. Buddy felt a sharp white heat go through his belly and out his back. He clenched his fists and jaws as tight as they would go and turned and walked over to the raw timber pile.

"That's enough." Andrew pulled a pencil from behind his ear and pointed to the pile of rough-sawn boards. "Get that loaded up and out of here, boys. And see if you can learn to talk less while you're traveling over to the store to sell this."

When the twins left, Andrew and Mac walked over to where Buddy was standing. He was muttering something.

"What?" Mac frowned, unsure of what he was hearing.

"If you can talk with crowds and keep your virtue, / Or walk with kings—nor lose the common touch, / If neither foes nor loving friends can hurt you, / If all men count with you, but none too much; / If you can fill the unforgiving minute / With sixty seconds' worth of distance run— / Yours is the Earth and everything that's in it, / And—which is more—you'll be a Man, my son."

Mac and Andrew stood looking at him with puzzled expressions.

"Rudyard Kipling," Buddy mumbled. "A man who knew how to be a man. I'm still trying. Really trying."

Andrew and Eva tried to keep a tight rein and close eye on Katie, especially since she was so beautiful, even as a small child, that she often struck people dumb. They made no apologies to anyone for their extreme protectiveness, rarely letting her out of their sight.

When Katie turned eleven and begged to go visit her school girl-friends, to stay the night with them, to roam the woods and fields to pick berries, Eva felt sorry for her and convinced Andrew that they could loosen the reins a little. They let her visit her friend Alice Lane by herself and even let her spend the night there. Alice was a quiet, sweet girl, never in any trouble, and an excellent student. Eva and Andrew felt comfortable that Katie and Alice would be nothing but good for each other. What the Teagues didn't know was that Alice's little brother, R.J.—Robert Jackson Lane—was a whole different story.

On those long, hot, sweet days that only children know, Katie, Alice, cousin Little Jim, and R.J. walked to their favorite fishing hole. On the way, they passed by a little house at the edge of the woods where the old man Henry Compton lived. Uncle Henry, as everyone always called him, was a constant source of speculation. When he was still able to get out and about, he wore many layers of clothes, even in summer, and he had the scariest eyebrows in the world, sprouting up like little exclamation marks above his eyes. As they walked by his house, R.J. would tell some of the local stories about Uncle Henry, how he never slept, how he could walk up behind someone with not a sound.

"People say they hear weird sounds coming from in there," R.J. whispered, looking over his shoulder at the house. "Some kids think he ain't real."

Katie and Alice nodded and looked back toward the house, too. They believed everything R.J. said.

The gang had devoted time and energy that spring to trying to get a look at Uncle Henry, or at least a good bragging story for the other kids. They'd seen his wife, Mary, only once when she came out to the mailbox one day. She'd hurried back up the yard when she saw the children and just made it inside and slammed the door as they reached the front of the house.

"She acted like she was plumb scared of us or something." Little Jim smirked.

One day, they'd put Little Jim up to sneaking up on the front porch and leaving a note, inviting Henry to go fishing with them. Another time, the boys had pelted his front door with stones, thinking he would come to the door and order them to stop. They wanted to see him and talk to him. But no one answered the door.

One evening they got the bright idea to roll a lot of kite string all over Henry's yard, looping it through the fence like a Christmas garland, throwing it over some small trees and shrubs. Then they ran like hounds and hid across the field to watch and wait. Again, no one responded.

"This is silly," Alice said. "I'm done fooling with this. Let's go play tag or something."

At supper that evening, Katie didn't have much to say, and Eva sensed something was on her mind. "What's the matter? Better eat that before it gets cold and you leave it for the cats. Are you not feeling well?"

"I'm fine. Just tired." Katie nibbled at some cornbread. "Does Uncle Henry Compton have any family, any kids or anything?"

"No children. One child was born dead and then they couldn't have no more. They was old when they married. It always grieved them. They always noticed other kids, you know, and Mary would give them candy and such. They made a fuss over you, how beautiful you are, and how you look just like your momma." Eva stopped herself, knowing that the mention of Alma was sure to cast a dark shadow over Katie's perfect face. "Why, honey? He ain't bothered you or anything, has he?"

"Oh, no. We tried to get him to go fishing with us, but they wouldn't even answer the door."

Andrew looked up from his food and spoke up. "Listen, Katie, y'all don't need to be bothering them. Henry ain't right. He shot his brother over some disagreement, shot him dead in the fields at their farm, with his sisters right there in the house."

Katie almost choked on her food. "What? Why isn't he in jail?"

"He was, for a long time, and then he got out. Listen, Katie, he's crazy as a loon, they say, and never has been right ever since he killed his brother. Now I never heard of him hurting anybody since or even threatening to, but I wouldn't push it. You all need to grow up and stop pestering people." Andrew slammed his coffee cup down harder than he meant to, and Katie's face turned red. He hadn't said a cross word to her more than a half-dozen times in his life. All of a sudden, Katie felt ashamed. She wanted to blame the boys because it was their idea, but she and Alice had gone along with them time and time again.

The next day, Katie told the gang what she'd learned at supper the night before. All of them were silent for a minute, and then R.J. whispered, "Damn." That was the end of pestering the old couple; none of them had to say it out loud—it was understood. They decided they'd walk to the store and see if old Mr. Blair would give them some free stick candy like he usually would. No one said anything more about Henry or Mary, but when the group came to the old dilapidated house in the bend of the road, they stopped and stared up at it. It gave them a thrill to look at a house that held a murderer and a woman who'd married a murderer.

"Howdy."

They jumped and looked around to see Aunt Becky Cain coming down the road toward them. She was the oldest person in the world, old as Methuselah, R.J. said. She was carrying a basket with flowers piled in it from her garden, and she had a stern look on her face that meant she had something to say. Mrs. Becky Cain always had something on her mind.

"Katie! R.J., what do you think you're doing?"

"We're just standing here talking." Alice smiled and stepped toward her.

"Don't you fib to me." She pushed her lined face down close to Alice, and the little girl stepped back.

"I heard about this, about you kids bothering them, trying to trick them into coming out." Mrs. Cain stood straight again.

Katie and Little Jim squirmed and stammered, and R.J. looked back down the road as if this conversation didn't involve him. Becky studied them, spit an amber star of tobacco juice in the dust, and squinted down at them with one eye shut.

"If you all did something besides pester, you'd know a thing or two. Henry's a sick man. Now why don't you kids find some work to do besides aggravation? Something pleasing to the Lord."

"Yes, ma'am," they all piped up together, and they said their goodbyes as quickly as they could. They didn't look back to see Becky watching them all the way until they disappeared over the hill. She stood and looked at the dusty footprints in the gravel, then up at the old house. She felt like she had grown up herself in that house, like a member of the family.

When she, Mary, and Henry were children, they had played there at Henry's house all the time, spent their summers together the way Katie and her friends did, running through the fields and woods, walking that porch railing, arms outstretched like circus performers, when her momma wasn't looking. Their bare feet stayed black as coal dust. She remembered the smell of the hyacinth at the edge of the steps mixed with the smell of wood smoke from the cookstove, and Henry's mother's cooked apples mixed with cinnamon. These were the smells of childhood for her, always, and she could close her eyes to this day and be back there, everything so real and close. Becky smiled at the memories, and just as she started to turn away, she saw an expressionless, gray face peeking out of one of the old windows. It was Mary, staring at her with dead eyes, like a goat. Becky raised her hand and then turned away toward home.

Meddling People

I am so aggravated I don't know what to do. I overheard Katie and Alice just chattering away out on the porch one day this week, and I got a shock. Alice was talking about her daddy promising to take her to the county fair this year for the first time and how excited she was. And then Katie says that Alice is lucky to have a daddy and how she's just not sure what to think about Ezra. Said that even if a body is sick, you'd think they'd come see their girl. I know Katie wrote him a letter a few months ago, but he hadn't answered it.

I know she's just a child and doesn't understand what it's like to be crippled up and almost destitute. For him to come see her would be a big undertaking, and he may not be able.

I hope I'm wrong but I can't help but be suspicious about what's got her thinking and talking that way about her daddy. Is it a coincidence that Buddy made some statement a week or so ago about "people who claim to be too sick to do their jobs and take on responsibility?" I remember he looked at Katie as he said it, and she stopped petting her kitten and looked off in the distance, lost in thought.

Gifts

I don't know what to make of Buddy Newman. I can't figure what he thinks. Some days he acts like he's in his own little world—if he talks much at all, it's only to Andrew. Other days he's in a big way, talking and laughing that crazy giggle of his and telling some of the funniest stories I ever heard. It's especially hot and cold with me. Sometimes I've caught him looking at me with the coldest, deadest stare, like he hates me or something. But of course, that's crazy. I ain't been nothing but kind, and Andrew even more so. Even with him trying to steal from us, we've treated him like kin.

Sometimes, he acts almost humble, almost teary-eyed, and thanks us all, tells us how much he appreciates having a roof over his head and a cooked meal. When he's in those moods, he'll bring me and Katie gifts. He's always bringing Katie apples—some of the Juneapples are getting ripe. He brought us wildflowers several times. He made Katie a doll out of cornshucks that was a woman holding a baby. It was amazing. Katie loved it. He promised he'd make her more, and he promised he'd show her how to make one herself. I bet he wishes he had some children of his own. He sure does dote on Katie.

He even offered to stay with her anytime we needed him or to go walk her home from school. I ain't never seen a man who wanted anything to do with babysitting, even though Katie isn't really a baby, but still. Most men don't want to fool with kids at all, but certainly not a girl, unless she likes to fish or something like that. I guess being all alone in this world like he is can change you, make you willing to do things you wouldn't normally do, to feel like you belong somewhere. But it could also be that Mr. Buddy Newman wants to take over everything around here and rule the roost, be in charge and tell all of us what's what. I may end up wishing he'd stole a chicken someplace else.

Worries

I don't know what I'm going to do now that Katie is getting big enough to want out of my sight. So far she has been such an easy child. She minds good. She does her homework and chores most of the time without anybody having to fuss at her. She's a joy and delight that brings a smile to everybody's face. But she's almost a teenager now, and kids get difficult then, some of them. They change into totally different people sometimes, wanting to rebel and fly out of the nest, wanting to court every boy or girl that comes along.

It worries me some that she draws so much attention. Katie is so beautiful that it's scary. I've seen how grown men react to her. It don't matter that she's just a child. From the time she was maybe 8 or 9, I've seen men do double-takes at her. Stop speaking in the middle of a sentence when she appears. Women think that being beautiful is the most wonderful thing—they'd take it over being rich. But it has its drawbacks. Women are jealous and men are hungry when they look at you. You are a big target.

Buddy's Tales

Buddy Newman is now like a regular member of our family. We don't only provide him a job and somewhere to sleep, but he eats here most of the time. Instead of three places, I have to set four at every meal. I don't know what to make of it. It ain't right. Andrew don't seem to see the extra work and expense he's took on. He's happy as a hog, walks around whistling to himself and talking more than he ever used to. It's like Buddy is the brother he never had. So I can't bring myself to say anything much to him, plus I know he wouldn't listen anyway. I want him to be happy. And Buddy never does seem to run out of stories. He's lived an amazing life.

Katie's Questions

It beat the life out of me, Katie wanting to know about Henry and Mary Johnson. What in the world goes on in a girl's head? I can't believe those kids were down there bothering them. And trying to get Henry to go fishing? That is just crazy.

I remember Mary from my childhood. It's strange to think how different she was then and how she is now. I haven't seen her in years and years. Nobody has, as far as I know. Back when I was a girl, she always came to church every time the doors were open. She smiled and laughed a lot, and she was very friendly, but in a quiet way. Her cooking was admired far and wide, and I once saw a church cakewalk where her cakes and pies brought the biggest price of all. When she went over there and moved in with Henry Johnson after he got out of the state mental hospital for killing his brother, it absolutely stunned everybody.

A group of women went over there from the church and tried to talk to her about what she was doing and about how it wasn't right that she was staying there with a man, a crazy one to boot, that she wasn't married to. But she'd offered them cherry pie, Reba Jones told everyone, and ignored everything they said. Then just two or three days later, they heard she'd called for Preacher Duncan to come to the house and marry them, and there she'd stayed.

Far be it from me to judge a lonely woman. When I met Andrew, here he was chasing my brother, possibly to hang him or at least put him in jail for a long time, and yet I dreamed about him. I spent my youthful years taking care of Momma and Daddy, and after my David died, I didn't have no way to meet a man and couldn't have done nothing with him if I found one. Mary was like me, tired of being alone, tired of waiting for her life to start, tired of not having a baby to hold like other women. She was tired, and Henry needed taking care of. I can't think about her no more right now. It makes me so very sad.

Dreaming

I've wondered a lot if other people dream like I do. I'm afraid to ask people because I know they'll want to hear about my dreams and such, and I can't tell anybody that. I can tell you, journal, and I guess that's what I want to do, to get it off my mind. I dream the weirdest, scariest stuff that mostly makes no sense. I dream of strange animals, of being naked in public, and being married to other people I barely know. Sometimes my dreams are so vivid and real and colorful that things look like drawings, except they're way, way better than anything I could ever draw.

Occasionally, I dream of horrible, gruesome violence—stuff I have never thought of when I was awake. It's nothing I want to write down or hold on to, but a teacher told us one time that we should keep a pencil and paper by our bed and try to immediately write dreams down as soon as we wake up, because we actually start to forget them the minute we wake up. She said they were a window on our soul and on our deepest desires and fears.

But if that's so, I can't see what in the name of heaven I want or am afraid of. It may be due to being too tired or something I'm eating. I know eating creasy greens and lots of green onions have led me to dream that monkeys lived in my henhouse, and another time, that a woman's hand came up out of the dirt of my garden, like it might if somebody was buried alive. I sat straight up in the bed and hollered out, covered in sweat. It was awful, so real.

The saddest mornings are the ones where I dream of David. I do not ever tell Andrew about these dreams. He would misunderstand, thinking I still loved David more, missed him, wished he was still here instead of me being with Andrew. That's not true. I would have loved for David to live to be an old man, and my baby, too, and we had all lived together all these years and watched that girl grow up to whatever she was going to be. But it wasn't meant to be. And loving David always in no way means I don't love Andrew, but he'd never understand that.

I dream the same dream oftentimes: David is walking away from me, out across the pasture with a garden hoe across his back, his right arm slung over the long handle to keep it steady. Then in the dream, I see him far off on the lower part of the farm, clearing some brush with a scythe, the high arc of the long, curving blade *creating a kind of slow-motion dance. He looks back at me one last time—for old times' sake, I always think in the dream—and then he turns and slowly walks away with his head down. He always turns one final time, not to look at me, but to look across the land, up to the top of Clinch Mountain, and then walks away. In the dream, I'm sobbing and calling his name, calling for him to come back, but then I wake up with a jerk. And I am glad it is a dream.*

One night at supper, Eva sat blowing across her coffee and sipping on it, watching Andrew above the cup's rim as he laughed and talked with Buddy about a childhood friend who was always getting into lots of "situations," as he called them. Andrew now talked to Buddy far more than he talked to Eva or Katie; in fact, it often seemed to Eva that he really would have been just as happy if they weren't there. The men talked about the mill, about equipment and how to best utilize it, about running a business and supervising workers, about things in the news. Most of all, they told each other stories.

"Have I told you about the time..." Andrew would ask almost every day, and Buddy would answer, "Why, no sir, I don't believe you have." He would sometimes give Eva a little grin, remembering she was there, if Andrew was telling a tale he'd told before. Eva heard stories she'd never heard: about the time his daddy's friend tricked him into getting on a wild pony that ran straight up a mountain and back down at breakneck speed, leaving Andrew hanging on for dear life, half-on, half-off the horse, only a handful of mane between him and the hard ground. He told about the haunted house where something grabbed him, about the ghost of a woman in a Big Stone Gap cemetery. Buddy would laugh and encourage another story and another until Katie and Eva gave up and washed the dishes. Sometimes the women would even go on up to bed to read, draw, or embroider, the men talking until at last their words became a light hum in the night, like a beehive.

Eva had gone up and was getting ready for bed on one of these nights when she heard a thump and then a commotion. Andrew ran to the foot of the stairs and called in a voice that immediately brought both Katie and Eva running.

"Something's happened to Buddy. He just fell over, out cold," he said, running back to the man who'd collapsed at his feet when he rose to say good night.

Buddy came to fairly quickly, but had no idea what happened. As soon as Eva touched him to help roll him over, she knew something was very wrong.

"He'd burning up, Andrew. He's bad sick."

Most people would have thanked their lucky stars that they woke up safe and sound in Katie's bed, which she had volunteered. She'd moved her things downstairs to a pallet she made for herself in the living room. Anyone else would have been so grateful for the sulfa drug that Eva and Andrew had the doctor send for Buddy, would have so appreciated having a safe, comfortable place in someone's home instead of shivering in a miserable fever in a stinking, muddy tent down at the jungle camp in Gate City. But Buddy was mostly just irritated.

"I ain't gonna stay here. It ain't right, and besides, I left things down there in Gate City that I don't want to git gone. If I don't get back there soon, they'll take 'em. No question."

"Listen, Buddy," Andrew said matter-of-factly. "I don't want to, but I'll stop you if you try to go. You need to take care of yourself and get well. You ain't hurting a thing by being here. Eva and Katie will watch over you, and you'll be back at work in no time. We can talk about you paying me back for the medicine then. I ain't worried about it and wouldn't even mention it at all, but I know how you are. I'm the same way, and I always expect to pay my own way and not be beholden to anyone."

Eva carried coffee and soup and eggs and toast up and down those stairs for a week. Buddy was sick enough that he was scared. His bed stayed soaked with perspiration; the fever would go away for a few hours, and he'd think the worst was over, only to have it return with such fierceness that the chills would leave him unable to talk or even stand. He would jerk violently and his teeth click together so hard that he feared they would break off.

Another man would have been humbled for the good care and generosity that surely saved his life. Being that sick in the filthy, cold camp in Gate City would have surely left him needing only a pauper's grave. But Buddy Newman was not one prone to gratitude. He felt it gave people a leg up on him; to be beholden to someone was to be in the weaker position. Buddy Newman liked people to owe him, not the other way around.

He snapped at Katie and Eva when they tried to wipe the sweat from his ashen face or offered to help feed him when he was too weak to sit up and do it himself. And he kept talking about something called "the black bottle." He seemed to think Eva or Andrew would give him some kind of medicine that would kill him, and his eyes would go wide and wild as a horse's that encountered a copperhead every time Eva came into the room with the sulfa drug the doctor had prescribed. She finally had to start hiding the medicine in a hot toddy of moonshine, honey, and coffee she gave him at bedtime.

"He thinks I'm trying to kill him or something, Drew. He's crazy, I'm telling you. He doesn't appreciate us. Not one bit."

Andrew just laughed. "He's out of his head with fever, Eva. He'll calm down when he gets to feeling better."

Buddy didn't act any nicer when he began to recover, though. When she would come in to check on him, he'd snap at her. "Get on!" he'd growl. "Can't a man get some peace?" He even wanted Katie to leave him alone, which was very unusual for him. He usually lit up when she walked into a room. After a few days, fatigue and irritation at his attitude finally got the best of Eva. She went up to his room, knocked lightly, and stepped inside.

Buddy was propped up a little in bed, looking out the window. He still appeared very weak, but he wasn't chilling as bad, nor was he wringing wet with perspiration as he had been so many times.

"Well, looks like you might have turned the corner." Eva smiled.

He gave her a blank stare and grunted. "I didn't call for you. I don't need nothin'."

"Well, I need something, Mr. Newman. I need for you to take a bath. It smells terrible in here." She didn't smile this time.

He sized her up. "Naw, I ain't able."

"Oh, you'll be fine. We'll get the water hot and bring you everything you need to wash up." She pushed back the curtains all the way and raised the window. "I'll set everything up over in our room. While you clean up, I'll change these nasty bedcovers."

He gave her a look that would have killed if it could. She could see he was thinking about cussing her or refusing, but he thought better of it.

When she got him situated in the other room with the bath underway, Eva began to clean up the filthy sickroom. She was trying to sweep when she accidentally knocked over his knapsack in the corner and things spilled out, including a stack of papers. Eva meant to just pick them up and stuff them back inside, but then realized they were drawings. Amazing drawings. She was rifling through the stack, marveling at the gift he had, the unique style, when she stopped and froze in horror. She felt as though time had stopped and she was outside her own body, watching herself. In her mind, she screamed out and put her hand to her mouth, but in a flash she realized she'd only imagined it.

There was a drawing of a beautiful young woman, naked, with the most perfect body you could imagine. She had long, thick, dark hair waving down, a single curl lingering beside erect nipples, the woman's own hand on the other breast. Her head was slightly back, and she was taking a bite out of a perfect apple, eyes closed. Though a few years older and more well developed, there was no mistaking her—it was Katie.

Eva slept little that night, replaying a thousand different ways of having a conversation with Andrew about Buddy and the drawing. But her certainty grew as the moon rose: Andrew wouldn't believe her. He would say it was her imagination, that Buddy wouldn't ever hurt Katie or anyone else, that artists had always drawn nude drawings of people and it wasn't anything bad. By the time the room began to go from black to gray, Eva had talked herself out of worrying about the drawing, pushed it to the place where she put all her dark worries.

One evening, it was unusually quiet at the supper table since Buddy had gone back into town to visit his friend at the Mission. Andrew had little to say to the women as Katie and Eva laughed about Katie's funny way of talking when she was a toddler and about some of her friends from school. His mind was a million miles away, to the point that he didn't hear the sound of someone coming up the step to the back door. After a light knock, Mac quickly poked his head into the room.

"Can a feller get a cup of coffee here?"

Eva jumped up and told him to take her seat, starting to fill a cup for him.

"Is something wrong?" Andrew wasn't used to Mac just dropping by. He had too much work to do, so he assumed there was some bad news. He dreaded to hear what it was. They couldn't handle a big repair bill of any kind.

"No, nothing really. I just wanted to talk to you about something if you have a few minutes." He looked at Katie and Eva with an anxious face. "I don't want to interrupt your meal. After you eat, maybe we can sit on the porch a spell."

Eva was curious about this odd behavior, but she didn't dare ask questions. She hustled Katie out of the way and left a fresh pot of coffee perking. Mac turned around and watched her move out of earshot before he said anything. But Eva stood behind the parlor door, her heart pounding. By tilting her head just so, she could see both men as well as eavesdrop on their conversation.

"Andrew, you know I'm pretty easy to get along with, and I sure ain't one to tell you how to run your business or who to hire." Mac stopped and cleared his throat. "But I felt like I had no choice. I wouldn't be a friend if I didn't say something about Buddy."

Andrew sighed. "Has he been disrespectful to you or not done what you tell him?"

"Not exactly. It's hard to explain. It's just that everything is different now." Mac stopped and sipped his coffee, appearing to ponder how to help Andrew see what was obviously true about the new hired hand. "Before he came, we all got along fine. None of the workers thought of either one of us as different, you know. They just worked alongside us, did what was needed usually without being told, cared about our work, and was just generally happy and easygoing. Now it's different."

"Wait now, Mac. I think I see this. Maybe you feel like I'm not as much of a friend to you as I have been. Because me and Buddy like to talk about things." He smacked Mac on the back and squeezed his shoulder. "You know, I think the world of you and couldn't run that business without you. That's a fact."

"No," Mac's jaw tensed. "Good Lord, Andrew, it ain't like I'm jealous or somethin'." Mac paused and rubbed his hand through his hair. He set his mouth in a straight line, trying to choose the right words. "No, this ain't anything like that. I know you and me are good. But he's a troublemaker. He runs me down and questions me to the others. He told Jonas that I thought I was some bigshot. And after I talked to the Clarks about taking their timber, he went to them and told them that some of the trees I'd said wasn't worth cutting were just perfect, and it was a shame I'd tried to get off cheap. It made me mad enough to cuss, Andrew." Andrew's stony silence and the stubborn set of his jaw seemed to stop Mac cold. Andrew always made it obvious when a conversation was over.

Mac set his coffee cup into the saucer gently and stood up. "I'm telling you this for sure, Andrew. He's a troublemaker. He likes to separate people, likes to run the show. And I'll tell you one last thing, but don't ask for no details about how I know: he's got no respect for women. None." He looked toward the two empty chairs where Katie and Eva had been sitting. "Just trust me on that one."

Eva quietly let out the breath she'd been holding. As Mac headed out into the twilight, she slipped off to the bedroom, where she spent a restless night of swirling questions with no easy answers.

The next day at the mill, Andrew started paying more attention to Buddy. He watched how he acted with the other men, how he acted when he talked to Andrew. It was true, what Mac had said. When he didn't know Andrew was observing him, Buddy looked different somehow. He seemed cocky. He stood ramrod straight and held his arms out from his sides as if he were a gunslinger waiting for somebody to draw their guns. Buddy said as little as possible to Mac, only what was necessary for work. When everybody stopped for dinner, Andrew went inside the little shed, saying he had to add up some figures, but he stepped around back where he could hear the men talking under the shade tree. Mac wasn't back there long at all. As soon as he finished a biscuit with a piece of ham on it that his wife had made for him, he came back around the shed and headed to the lumber pile.

Buddy was alone with Jacob and Joshua, and Andrew heard them start snickering. "Did you make this?" one of them asked. Andrew couldn't make out Buddy's answer. "Oh my God. I ain't never seen nothing like that in my life. Look at her!"

Buddy must have changed positions because now Andrew could hear him clearly when he said, "Yeah, I keep lots of them kind of girlies in my pocket, right close to where I want 'em." And at that the twins howled and started describing in detail what was obviously a naked female, well-endowed and in a very explicit position. *He's got to be talking about one of those nickels he carries,* Andrew thought to himself. *He couldn't have drawings in his pocket.* Andrew remembered Buddy giving Katie one of those nickels he carved. When he got home, he'd ask Katie about them.

Andrew brooded and fumed the rest of the day. *Mac and Eva see something I don't.* Andrew scratched his head and wondered what he was missing that everyone else could see so plainly. He left for home puzzled, questioning how a person could have so many faces, so many selves, and how anyone could figure it all out.

16

When Nancy Lawson turned forty, all of a sudden she had to be touched. She'd been alone all her life. She caught herself sometimes, sometimes not, when she found herself touching people at any opportunity—her sister, Mrs. Blair down at the store, the people she'd be talking to at church.

She'd made a fool out of herself over her doctor the year before. Dr. Arnold was so handsome and kind. He wore bowties—something Nancy just loved—and had the softest voice, a warm smile. She daydreamed about him like a schoolgirl. When she finally got up the nerve to ask him to do a complete checkup, she fretted herself into a frazzle by the time he came into the examining room.

When he got close enough to listen to her heart, to look into her eyes and ears, she had to fight to keep her breathing under control. When he had her lie back so he could press on her abdomen, she felt her skin go to gooseflesh. She tried to listen to his explanations and questions, but was unable to stop her eyes from closing, her mouth from forming in a soft round "O" as he tried to explain what a breast exam was. Nancy had let out a little moan then, and Dr. Arnold had just given his nurse a flustered look and left the room. The nurse finished with a few more questions, patted Nancy's hand, and left.

Nancy had been so mortified that her face stayed red until sometime the next day. She never went back. But that embarrassment didn't deter her search for love and her hunger for touch; it had only grown more urgent lately.

At church last week, Brother Hiram Qualls, elder at her church, had just laid his hand on her back and patted it as she knelt at the altar, and her skin had tingled and moved all over, her face growing hot. When she went to the store later in the week, Alfred Taylor had put his arm around her shoulder and told her how grateful he was for the food she brought by when his mother died. Nancy caught herself closing her eyes to feel that strong arm and think about how nice it would be to have it there on a regular basis. As she talked to Alfred, she noticed another man that she hadn't seen before, one with dark curly hair and big eyes.

He looked at her as if he knew exactly what she was thinking, and it startled her, made her face flush. She stepped away from Alfred's arm and stammered about how it was her pleasure and all, jostling bags of candy that were on a rack by the door. When they began to fall, Alfred and the dark-haired man rushed to pick them up, and when the candy had all been returned to the rack, Nancy straightened up to find herself not a foot from those eyes, crinkled at the corner, his lips curled into a little smile.

"Careful, ma'am," he drawled in a voice so deep and soft it felt like fingers touching her as he spoke.

When she left the store, he was standing at the edge of the road lighting a pipe.

"My name's Buddy Newman, ma'am. I just started work at Nettles' Sawmill. Are you going that way?" She wasn't, but decided there must be someone she could visit that way.

"I... I've heard of you. You're the drifter working at the sawmill. I've heard that you're very talented. The Dockery twins' aunt was telling me about your artwork at church." She smiled up at him. Buddy flashed her the sweetest smile and stared deep into her eyes as he talked to her.

They walked and made small talk, but only for a few minutes. Talking to Buddy Newman was like nothing else she'd ever experienced. He asked strange questions: "Do you like pumpkin pie? What was the first fish you ever caught? Do you like poetry?"

She started to tell about her fourth grade teacher, Miss Marple, whose reciting of Shakespeare used to send them all into barely controllable giggles because of her speech impediment, but Buddy stopped in the middle of the road and locked eyes with her again as he begin reciting:

> "No—yet still steadfast, still unchangeable,
> Pillowed upon my fair love's ripening breast,
> To feel forever its soft fall and swell,
> Awake forever in a sweet unrest,
> Still, still to hear her tender-taken breath,
> And so live ever—or else swoon to death."

"It's Keats," he said, tapping his pipe against a bony palm. Nancy stood with her mouth open, like a baby or a puppy looking at something to eat, perspiration breaking out along her hairline and a feeling in her stomach she'd never felt before.

Buddy Newman found out Nancy went to one of the little local Baptist churches. So the next Sunday morning, he asked Andrew if he might borrow a horse for the morning to go to the Mission in Gate City and attend services there. Andrew tried to get him to go to the local Methodist Church that he and Eva attended, but Buddy insisted he'd be more comfortable worshiping with his own kind at the Mission. Andrew gave in and off Buddy went on Eva's horse. Instead of Gate City, he turned down the road toward Nancy's church.

Buddy burst in on horseback through the open double doors of the church just as the service was getting started. He spotted Nancy sitting in the middle section of the rows of benches, singing along with the opening hymn. A boy turned and whispered something to his mother, and Nancy locked eyes with Buddy for a long moment.

Several women screamed and the preacher froze, his eyes big as silver dollars, the horse stomping and pawing and sliding on the wood floor. A little boy near the back of the church began to cry loudly. Buddy looked alarmed and wild-eyed himself, but he finally got the horse to stand still. Some men from near the front stepped out into the aisle, instinctively reaching inside their coats for guns they had left at home. Buddy hopped off the horse quickly and removed his hat.

"Mercy, I'm… I'm sorry, folks. I didn't mean for this to happen. I don't know what got into this fella."

He looked from face to face, to the men in the front who looked ready to jump him, to the women who were pale as the pages of the songbooks in their hands. He could see that many of them had no idea who he was, but their curiosity had been piqued at the identity of this tall, rugged man with his smooth tanned skin and shock of curls.

"I'll take care of any damages. I'm just going to ease him back out of here." Buddy began to push on the animal's head, backing him through the door. Right before he went out, he stopped and turned and tipped his hat to them. "Ladies, sorry for the scare." He fastened those eyes, dark as a cave, on Nancy Lawson and let a tiny smile curl up one side of his lips. Her face flushed bright red.

When Buddy got far enough away that he knew he was safe, he threw his head back and laughed and laughed until the tears came. Then he wrote a little note that said: "You cannot conceive how I ache to be with you, how I would die for one hour… by John Keats" and left it in her mailbox as he rode on to Gate City to see if his money had come. This was always so delicious, this anticipation, the plotting, the chase. The flashing image of her pinned under him, wide-eyed and warm.

He now had two games going, and he felt more alive than he had in years. While Nancy was a fun side game, he hadn't wavered in his larger purpose—getting Katie under his control. After Buddy had followed the children a few times and learned of their fascination with Mary and Henry Johnson, it occurred to him that he could use Katie's interest in them to his benefit. Almost everything he heard, in fact, was filed away and analyzed to see if it could be used to accomplish his objective: to earn everyone's trust, especially Katie's, and to pull closer or develop some leverage over Andrew and Eva. To get someone to fully drop their defenses and instincts for safety and self-protection took planning and cunning. Buddy lived for the game.

One evening after supper while Eva gave Andrew a haircut outside, Buddy and Katie stayed behind in the kitchen to play a game of checkers. She loved to play, and Buddy almost always let her win. He had her convinced she was the best checker player he'd ever seen.

"I heard Eva say you'd been going out to visit with that Mary Johnson, the one who's crazy. Why you doing that?"

Katie's face darkened and pulled into a tight frown of disapproval. "She's not crazy. Just lonely and sad. You would be, too, if you stayed in the house all the time with somebody really crazy and sick." The frown was replaced by a big grin as she did a double-jump and took two checkers.

"Well, excuse me, Miss Hotshot!" Buddy waved his arms and shook his head, making Katie giggle at his dramatics over her winning move. "I guess you're right. I think Andrew said they married late and had a baby, but something was wrong with it. That'll make anybody sad and crazy." Buddy dropped his head and pretended to wipe his eyes. Katie frowned again.

Buddy acted as though he was a little embarrassed. "I... I don't talk about it. I really regret not having any kids of my own. That's the main business of life, and I missed it. I missed it." He didn't look at Katie.

She reached over and laid her hand on the back of his. "That's sad, Buddy. Maybe you'll just have to be like Auntie and Drew—adopt me." She smiled the smile that filled rooms and patted his hand again. Buddy looked down at the beautiful hand on his own and brought his other hand down on top of it. He held her hand in his and squeezed and patted it. "Yes, sweet girlie, maybe so. You're a good girl."

Katie pulled her hand from his and soon took more checkers off the board, smiling to herself. She arranged the captured checkers in perfect stacks with her fingers, and Buddy studied her hands.

"I know one thing for sure, little girlie: if I had a little girl like you, I wouldn't go off and leave you like your daddy has. That's for certain."

Katie's brow wrinkled and she stared at him hard, but said nothing. She began to wring her hands, and she looked over at a framed photograph of her father standing beside his brothers and sisters when they were all children. Buddy could read her thoughts, watching her from the corner of his eye, and he was thrilled with the way things were progressing. Katie was pretty much wrapped around his finger, and Nancy wanted to be. He was on top of the world.

17

Buddy wasn't taking his eyes off the prize—oh no, that wouldn't happen—but meeting Nancy Lawson created an interesting sideline that definitely held his interest. He hadn't had a woman in a long time. *She's a ripe one. She'll be juicy and sweet.* Buddy chuckled to himself.

He'd already sized her up and figured his chances were slim as long as he was only some hobo who'd showed up to work at the sawmill. He'd arrived at the grim conclusion that his only shot might be to start going to church with her and pretend he'd found Jesus. That ruse had always worked for him, but he hated it. He could only get through it by imagining the women and girls without their clothes. He absolutely hated the preachers—he always thought of them as the "holier-than-thou holy rollers." He'd like to hold the head of every single one of them in the creek and watch them stop bubbling.

So when the men at the sawmill mentioned there was going to be a supper, talent show, and cakewalk at the local school to raise money for some repairs and improvements, Buddy was thrilled. He'd kept a low profile in Wayland, but here was a chance to use his gifts to a larger purpose. He grinned at his good fortune.

Saturday night, everybody showed up at the school. The women brought food they set up on long tables out under a shade tree. Anyone could eat for a donation. Eva, Andrew, and Katie arrived, all of them scrubbed clean, Katie with a big red bow in her hair. Buddy sat near them in the shade while they all ate. He didn't say much because Katie and her friend Alice sat together, talking a mile a minute. Buddy knew this was a good time to gather information, anything at all he could use later to pull Katie closer.

Off to one side, a table held cakes and pies of all kinds. Four old men sprawled under a shade tree with fiddles and banjos, practicing a tune. People from Gate City and other communities had come because they wanted to compete in the talent show and win the prize from local store owner Mr. Blair.

In a little while, people would line up in a big circle. They had placed little slabs of wood on the ground with numbers on them. You would walk around that circle while the musicians played, and everybody would stop when the music stopped. Then someone drew numbers out of a bucket. If they drew the number a contestant stood beside, the lucky person won a cake. Then the music would start again. Everyone would go round and round, put their nickel in the collection box, and after everyone had paid, the music would stop again. Everyone laughed and shouted when a winner was chosen, along with handing out much teasing about cheating, about not needing to eat more cake, about wanting to win a certain woman's cake, and so on. The children scuffled and grinned, trying to push each other off numbers when the music stopped, and the mothers let them as long as they didn't get too rowdy. People were happy to be together, happy for a chance to see people they rarely saw.

Buddy was sick of this wholesome cornball party within half an hour of arriving, but his heart leapt when he saw Nancy in the crowd, placing what looked to be a perfect lattice-topped pie on the table. When she looked up, he smiled at her and winked. She flushed a little and walked over to where he stood leaning against an oak tree.

"Why, good evening. Didn't expect to see you here."

"Oh, I wouldn't be anywhere else tonight, Miss Nancy, than to be where I might get to see a smile as beautiful as yours, or maybe get a chance to win a pie like that." He gestured toward the dessert table.

Nancy flushed a deeper red and burst out with a girlish giggle. "Oh, well, good luck, Mr. Newman." And with that, she moved toward the women at the food table.

Buddy, Eva, Andrew, Katie, and Alice rose and walked a few rounds, dropping their nickels into the box over and over. It didn't take them long to walk off all the desserts. Then the school principal got up and addressed the crowd. People revered Mr. Fugate, a tall, imposing man with a slight lisp, and they were grateful for his leadership at their school. He spoke eloquently and everyone listened. He had a different accent from theirs, though he never made an issue of it with the children. He did insist on correcting their grammar, but always with a smile, insisting that proper use of language in speech fed directly into proper writing, which was extremely important.

Most of the parents had little to no formal education, but they were proud to have their children and grandchildren at the "big school," as everyone called it. Most of them walked in and looked around that evening, many for the first time, marveling at the high ceilings and the books, the children's drawings on the wall. The school had only been built a few years ago. They couldn't imagine what it would have been like to have such a childhood. They'd been putting aside a little money, even the poorest among them, to come to this event and help the school. It was a new day in Wayland, and they were all hopeful for the future.

Buddy paid careful attention to his face and posture, staying in his smiley, people-pleasing, country-boy stance. When they called for the talent show signup to begin, a crowd quickly gathered around the table. The audience would pick the winner by applause, and the top performer would receive ten dollars' worth of free merchandise from the store. That would be a help to any family's food budget, and it was a fortune to the children: the little girls dreamed of the beautiful dolls the store had every Christmas, while the boys envisioned toy trucks and marbles and BB guns.

The show was a wonder. Many of the young girls got up and sang hymns. Two boys showed off their fantastic buck-dancing skills on a little wooden platform they'd brought, with Uncle John, the local fiddler, playing a fast tune as their work boots tapped out an amazing rhythm that rang off the boards. Mostly, the contestants were musicians—people played harmonica, fiddle, autoharp, dulcimers. Several kids stood up and recited poems. Buddy applauded loudly for all of them. When it was his turn, he walked slowly to the front, individuals in the crowd looking at each other, wondering what in the world he would do. He didn't have an instrument, and he didn't look like a dancer.

He cleared his throat. "Ladies and gentlemen, thank you for allowing me to be a part of this wonderful evening with all of you. I'd like to take this opportunity to do a little performance I've done all over the country. It's a recitation of a passage from one of our country's great books, *The Adventures of Huckleberry Finn* by Mr. Mark Twain, whose real name was Samuel Clemens."

At this point, audience members exchanged little bemused grins; this wasn't what they'd expected. But their faces showed surprise at his words and the way they were delivered. Buddy knew most of them had no idea who he was, and that those who knew thought he was no more than a sad hobo down on his luck, uneducated and penniless. They must realize now that he'd fallen far in life.

"In Mr. Clemens' book, there's a crazy character called 'The Child of Calamity' who entertained people he met with outrageous bragging and hyperbole." Buddy stopped and smiled, gauging the crowd's reaction. Most looked either puzzled or poker faced. He pressed on. "If you've ever heard the children's tale of Paul Bunyan, you have some idea of where Twain got the idea. It's a classic tradition in American tales, and I'd like to perform part of one of 'The Child of Calamity' speeches here tonight. I hope you enjoy it."

Buddy paused and cleared his throat. Then he rocked back on his heels, grabbed the lapels of his jacket, and hollered out, "Whoop!"

Some of the women jumped, and the children giggled.

"I'm the old original iron-jawed, brass-mounted, copper-bellied corpse-maker from the wilds of Arkansaw. Look at me! I'm the man they call Sudden Death and General Desolation!" Buddy had changed his voice to be more gruff, more country.

The men began to grin at one another, and boys elbowed the boy next to them.

"Sired by a hurricane, dam'd by an earthquake, half-brother to the cholera, nearly related to the smallpox on the mother's side! Look at me!"

At this point, many began to chuckle.

"I take nineteen alligators and a barrel of whiskey for breakfast when I'm in robust health, and a bush of rattlesnakes and a dead body when I'm ailing. I split the ever-lasting rocks with my glance, and I squench the thunder when I speak! Whoop!"

He threw his head back and hollered again, and at this the crowd erupted, forgetting themselves and their bad teeth or what the neighbors might think. Everyone was laughing, old and young, shaking their heads and muttering to each other how that was the funniest thing they'd ever heard.

"Stand back and give me room according to my strength! Cast your eye on me, gentlemen! And lay low and hold your breath, for I'm about to turn myself LOOSE!"

The crowd was laughing so raucously now that they probably didn't hear all of the rest of it clearly, about how he scratched his head with lightning bolts and sucked the clouds dry like a sponge when he was thirsty.

Buddy was enjoying himself, reveling in his success, but he had to make himself stop. He could have quoted the whole scene from the book, but he'd reached his goal.

Nancy was also looking around and laughing, dabbing the corners of her eyes with her little handkerchief. She beamed at him, like a proud family member might do. Buddy felt giddy enough to wink at her and smile.

When Mr. Fugate called them all up and asked the crowd to applaud as each name was called, it wasn't close at all. Buddy was the winner without question. Mr. Blair came up front and gave him a little piece of paper explaining that he could have ten dollars' worth of free merchandise at the store, and everybody applauded again, and the other contestants patted him on the back.

As soon as the hubbub died down, Buddy went straight to Nancy and said, "I did this for you. Just go pick you out what you want. Maybe some cloth for a new dress or something. I don't need nothing but a smile from you."

"That's so sweet of you. Come over sometime and we'll talk about it." Nancy patted his arm. "And since you didn't win my pie, I'll make another one just for you."

Buddy walked out of there and back to his little room at the mill happier than he'd been in a long time.

18

Buddy was now the most popular man in Wayland after some of the preachers, teachers, and musicians. They put the tale of riding the mule into the church with his talent show performance.

"He's a prankster," they laughed, "like old Zeke Quillen used to be."

People knew talent when they saw it and certainly appreciated anyone who could make them laugh like that. It was extra special because he made them laugh together. In times as hard as they had seen, as hard as life was, as lonely and stressful and fragile, it was something to treasure, a rare moment when they could all be in one place and totally abandon themselves to shared delight. Once in a while, a preacher might be funny enough to elicit a shared laugh, but certainly with nothing of the unselfconscious, raucous joy of that evening.

Everybody wanted to know more about Buddy. When he went to the store now, the group of old men who sat on the porch most days called out to him, offering him a spot on their bench. Some of them had heard from the Dockery twins about the famous "hobo nickels" he carved, and they wanted to see one. He made sure not to show them any of the ones with the vulgar depictions of women. Like everyone else, they were amazed and impressed with his talent.

Buddy played it all to the hilt, of course, because the more everyone bragged on him, the more attention it would get from Nancy Lawson. She was the prize. He had to convince her that he was no different from any other man she might meet, and he had to make sure she forgot he lived in the squalid hobo jungle in Gate City, that he was considered the lowest of the low—a "tramp."

Nancy soon fell for it completely. She started inviting him over for supper and even invited him to a Sunday gathering at her sister's house. Buddy was nervous about this. He hated being at the disadvantage, not knowing who the players were, not knowing what kind of obstacle or trap might present itself when he entered unknown territory like this. But he pressed on. The prize would be worth the risk.

He didn't want to have to take her by force, since he wasn't ready to leave Wayland yet. If he had been, he would just do what he'd done before in similar circumstances: he'd show up late one night and knock on her door, pretending to have some sort of problem he needed her help with, and then do what he wanted when he got inside. But that only worked when he was ready to hop a train and be long, long gone when the woman got over the shock of what happened. No, he wanted to seduce Nancy and let her try to say it wasn't what she wanted. He chuckled to himself when he thought of it.

Buddy spent several weeks making sure everybody knew they were courting. He took her on a picnic and joined her at the local tent revival. That was enough of an irritation to lead him to make his move. He asked her to pack another picnic and go down to the river with him. They'd pass a nice day together enjoying nature. He laughed to himself as he thought of it: *Yes sir, we'll really enjoy nature, just nature taking its course.*

Even though Eva couldn't see the attraction, other women took notice of Buddy Newman, especially after the school talent show. He was now one of the most popular people in Wayland. They all watched him and smiled at him, expected him to be funny, asked him to say part of his speech again. Eva had been astonished on several occasions to see respectable, happily married women start to sway back and forth, touch their own hair, talk in a babyish voice in Buddy's presence, or touch his arm while they talked with him. Eva felt embarrassed for them.

So when her husband told her about the gossip down at Blair's Store, she was not nearly as surprised by it all as he was. It seemed "Uncle Albert" Smith, the local beloved sot who was the star of many a funny story, had caught one of the "old maids" of the community in a very compromising position with Buddy down on the river bank.

Everybody had a real soft spot for Albert, but talked about him and his crazy family all the time. They were the strangest bunch. If any one of them had anything important to do, whether it was go to the bank, the doctor, or the voting precinct, they all went together—Albert, his three brothers, and his daddy. People almost never saw them say a word to each other, yet it was as though they read minds. One brother might look over at one of the others, and he'd reach in his pocket for the supplies and roll him a cigarette. Their house had Bible verses written all over the walls in one of its rooms, and the other one had all kinds of strange drawings. Nobody knew which one of the brothers was the artist.

Uncle Albert, who was nobody's uncle as far as anyone knew, was most famous for making young girls scream and run away from him outside the store. He'd make a beeline for any pretty young girl he saw as long as she was marrying age—sixteen or so. Albert couldn't quite talk plain, and lots of the boys got a big kick out of mimicking his speech. Because he was known far and wide to not be "quite right," he got away with stuff that any other man would have been slapped in the face for. He'd sidle up beside the young girl or a married woman—all the same to him—hold his index finger up in the air, and say, "Eh girl, 'et's you and me go, one time, just one time." He'd never gotten out of hand, never touched anyone or anything like that, but many of the older women stared him down, and a few had even told him off for acting that way. Albert would act all serious and say, "Now, I'd jus' jokin', ain't no harm in me." After they left, he'd cackle about it and tell the men standing in a circle spitting tobacco juice or smoking what the women said.

According to Uncle Albert's latest tale, he'd taken a fishing pole and a sandwich and was having a fine afternoon down on the Clinch River seeing if he could catch something he could eat. He took a break, leaving his pole wedged in the forks of a tree, and walked down the bank, happily eating his sandwich. When he came around a little bend, he found himself suddenly almost on top of Buddy Newman, who was completely on top of "a local lady," Albert said. The woman's eyes had grown big as quarters when she spotted Uncle Albert over Buddy's shoulder, and when she let out a scream, Buddy and Albert both screamed, too, and Buddy jumped up. Albert had to jump back, and he lost his footing in the soft loam of the river bank. He went down on one knee in the muck, his sandwich hitting the water with a soft *plop!*

"I'm… I'm sorry," he said. "I didn't mean to be here." He looked down at the water. "Dang it—you done ruint my damn sandwich."

Albert then turned away before they could react and walked as fast as he could back to his fishing spot. Behind him he heard the woman's muffled sobs and the comforting murmur of Buddy's voice as they straightened and gathered themselves. Albert grabbed his fishing pole and hightailed it out of there. He didn't know Buddy Newman that well, but he knew enough to be scared of him. That man had a look in his eye that Albert was sober enough to fear.

But the next time he got a little whiskey in him and a good audience, he told the story, withholding the woman's name "out of respect," he said. "He must have sweet-talked or tricked her some way. I ain't one to bring no shame on nobody." And he kept telling the story when he saw what a big laugh it got, embellishing it and perfecting the wording each time. Depending on who was in the audience, the details and description became more graphic, more crude. He'd make sounds he claimed Buddy Newman had been making and finally began describing his anatomy.

"I felt kinda sorry for 'im. He ain't got nothin' down there. Hit weren't no bigger than a carpenter's pencil."

The men in the circle howled and slapped each other on the back. They begged for more details, especially about Buddy's partner. But Albert stuck to his guns on that one and his look went all serious. "No sir, I ain't tellin'. It's bad enough she got to live with it."

Buddy's previous escapades had set tongues wagging, but now the gossip generated by Uncle Albert's telling had really created a sensation. Wayland hadn't had such a scandal since Virgil Elliot left his wife for the Slant schoolmarm and they disappeared into the night the week after school let out.

Eva listened to her husband's bemused account of running into Uncle Albert during one of his performances at the store and chuckled a little at Uncle Albert's way of telling the tale. But Eva also knew this would add fuel to the fire, something she could use to get Andrew to finally realize Buddy wasn't all he was cracked up to be.

"See what I mean, Andrew? He's just sleazy. I don't trust him a bit. I don't like having somebody around here who generates that kind of gossiping! It ain't good for your business either, honey."

"Everybody ain't a choir boy, Eva. I'll talk to him about it—see what he says about it all. Don't you worry." He nuzzled her hair and kissed her cheek.

"It just don't make sense to me, Andrew. I can't imagine, don't want to imagine." She leaned in close to her husband and whispered, even though they were the only ones in the room. "I won't say who, but a person not given to carrying false tales had already told me about it, and they said it was Nancy Lawson. Nancy Lawson out on a riverbank! What in the world? That just don't sound like her at all, Drew."

"People are crazy in love, you know that. It'll make fools out of a preacher or scholar just the same as any of us." He shrugged and started putting on his boots. "Let me handle it. Don't you talk it to nobody. You don't know what's true. No use being part of the gossiping."

She actually thought no more about the story, or Albert, or any of it, just pushed it out of her mind, until one day a week later a group of ladies from her church showed up on her front porch with a pound cake. Eva had just come out on the porch to sit down and fan herself after the work of the midday meal. Andrew had gone back to the sawmill, and Katie was still at school. The visit surprised her enough, but the cake was especially puzzling. *Did they think somebody had died or was sick?*

Annabelle Hensley, Margaret McConnell, and Mildred Stewart called "Hello" and "Can you visit a spell?" and "Aren't your flowers beautiful!"—talking all at once as they stepped up onto the porch in Sunday dresses.

"Well, how wonderful!" Eva said. "What brings you all out here? And with one of Annabelle's delicious cakes? Did somebody tell you I'd finally killed Andrew for being so sassy?" Eva laughed, but the women didn't.

They only smiled strained smiles, and Mildred cleared her throat. "No, we came to talk to you about you and Buddy Newman."

19

Hobo College

Buddy was telling us the biggest tale yet. He said they had something they called Hobo College. In the bigger cities, like Knoxville, there are so many hobos, and lots of them are actually educated people with college degrees and fancy jobs and everything, but for whatever reason they wind up as hobos. Anyway, he says they have debates about everything—politics, the Bible. Maybe that explains how he knows so much about everything. I swear, I've been amazed myself a few times. Katie thinks he's some kind of genius. She's all the time coming across something in her reading or school work and saying, "Oh, I'll have to ask Buddy about this." He knows art, history, poetry—you name it. He can quote things off the top of his head, things that are just right for whatever occasion or whatever conversation you're having. He's really something else. To have his natural talent at so many things, but most especially his greatest gift, drawing, is really something miraculous.

More about Buddy

I was thinking more about Buddy and the talent show and the tales he tells. He is, I have to admit, one of the smartest people I ever met. He has a natural talent to draw better than anyone I know, and he is as well read as people like Principal Fugate or old Miss Marple. It's obvious he's read a lot of books, and more important, seems to be able to remember every word of them!

If you have that kind of ability and natural, God-given gifts, why would you end up like he has? Why isn't he a principal or a college professor somewhere? Why doesn't he have a family and beautiful home to call his own? No, something is wrong with this picture. Now I know these hard times have put many a good, hard-working man on the street and on rock bottom. But here's the thing: the ones as smart as him, they get back on their feet pretty quick. Think about it: what job out there could he not do if he wanted to? Just the more I learn about him, the more I study him, the more certain I am that there's something wrong with him. It's obvious to everybody who knows quite a bit about him—well, except Andrew, that is.

Friendships

I have just been at wit's end with this whole thing about Andrew and Buddy, trying to think how I could get Andrew to wake up and see the light. And it got me to thinking about how men and women are so different when it comes to friendships. Women have only maybe 2 or 3 close friends, at most, and they confide everything to each other, keep each other's secrets. Men often call their friends their "buddies," but they may never talk to each other much at all. They just have something in common they like to do, and that makes them instant friends.

My daddy's best friend was Grady Jones—they were closer than brothers. They loved to go fishing together and build things. That's it. And at least when I was ever around, they didn't talk to each other much at all. But if Daddy had a big job to do around the farm or it was planting time, Grady was right there by his side. They just talked about the task at hand. Of course, I guess it's possible that out there on the riverbank with the river trickling by and the breeze singing in the trees, maybe they poured out all their worries and stories to each other. I don't know.

All I know is I can't imagine having a woman friend that only came around to do some work, like planting flowers, and not talk about nothing else. Just say, "Where do you want these zinnias?" or "Hand me that rake, would you?" and that's it. But it seems to me that's what men do.

Maybe that's why they can be fooled the way Andrew is. They keep everything on the surface, don't let things get too deep.

Praying

I wish I could pray the way some preachers can, just roll off pieces of the Psalms, phrases from the Song of Solomon or Paul's letters, rolling off the tongue like music, like the waterfall down at the Foam Hole on Copper Creek. I wish I had the gift of words like that. I feel like if you're going to talk to God hisself, you ought to have something beautiful to say, not grate and whine. I've worked and worked on this, wasted several sheets of paper. I couldn't remember it, so I just read it to God a while ago, and I already feel a peace about it.

Dear Lord, I come to You worn and bone-tired, trudging through life's troubled waters today. I'm looking up to the hills from whence cometh my help, like the Good Book says, where You watch over us all. I need shade from the heat of worry and fear, a restful sleep under a quilt of dreams and mercy, sweet Father, so I can rise into morning's sweet silence a new woman, or better yet, my old self, but happy. I need Your guidance and strength to lift me, Lord, as I try to see my way free of bonds my mistakes have chained me to. In Jesus precious name—Amen.

Nosy Women

I cannot believe some women. They run around with their noses out of joint—either they got them turned up in the air looking down on you because you ain't as pretty, or dressed as nice, or have as fine a house, or they got it run into your business, being a busybody telling you how to live. They showed up out here insinuating that I ought not have Buddy Newman sitting with his feet under my supper table on account of his fooling around with some woman on the riverbank. One of them had the nerve to say "some people" might even speculate something was going on between me and him with him hanging around here all the time.

I got so mad my hands were jerking. I had to set my coffee cup down. I told them by that logic they might think every man that worked for my husband was diddling with me, or maybe it was the man we bought hay off of, or old Mr. Blair down at the store. I thought Anna Belle was going to have a heart attack. Her face turned purple. As I was saying it, I walked toward the front door and opened it. "I appreciate you dropping by. I'm sure I wouldn't want to keep you from your other visits. I'm sure they's lots of places you're needing to stop." You could have cut the air with a knife. They stomped out of there and down those steps like soldiers in a drill. Gossipy old bags! I guarantee they ain't nobody talking about me and Buddy Newman except them!

Changing My Mind

Well, Journal—I take back what I said. I have learned more that has me quite uneasy and concerned. It turns out the woman on the riverbank was Nancy Lawson, for true! I can't hardly believe it, but the person that told me was certain and wouldn't lie about such a thing, though I won't name her here. I just know something isn't right. Nancy wouldn't act like that, for just the very bad thing that happened: there's no way she would ever in a million years put herself in a position to be caught out in broad daylight doing such as that.

Nancy comes from very proper and upstanding people, and a long line of preachers and Sunday School teachers, to boot! I have this sick feeling about the whole thing. And when I add it to the other things I've seen out of Buddy, it makes me sick to my stomach. I think he's a bad man, with no regard for anybody but his own selfish self. Nothing matters to him except what he wants.

And then there's Katie. She seems different somehow. I know she's getting older and it may just be the growing pains of becoming a young woman, but then I hear Buddy saying little things against the church and God, planting ideas in her head that ought not be there. I don't like it. Not one bit.

20

Katie wasn't sure what was happening to her, but something was definitely different. She felt confused and on edge, and her mind raced. Her dreams had become vivid and complicated. At times she felt angry at Eva and Andrew for no real reason. They could tell her to do something or talk to one another and ignore her like she wasn't there, and she wanted to scream at them. She told herself sometimes that no one cared about her and that she should just run away. She even packed up a little sack, like Buddy had told her about all the hobos doing.

Yet all the time she was doing these things, there was another person, the old Katie, that kept telling her, *You know this isn't right. You have a good life. You've been so blessed.* She knew Aunt Eva and Uncle Drew had taken good care of her, made sure she had everything she needed and some nice things, too, more than most of her schoolmates had, and when those dark thoughts passed, she felt guilty and even more confused. At times, she scared herself.

Buddy watched Katie closely and read the confusion and the adolescent moods with delight. He fed it at every opportunity. He told her all about his travels and his learning, slipping in little asides about how Eva and Andrew probably didn't know about these things. When he'd pushed that as far as he dared and could see in Katie's eyes that she looked up to him and trusted him, he decided to make a little strike against her dad. Since Ezra wasn't around, he couldn't really threaten Buddy's plan, but this game was a big part of the fun.

One day he struck up a conversation with Katie about his drawings and the hobo nickels and how happy it made him to be able to do it. He'd brought her one of the last good Juneapples from the neighbor's pasture.

"Have you ever tried drawing? I bet you could. Your Aunt Eva can. And I think your daddy was a talented fellow, too. Did he draw?"

"No, not as far as I know. He liked to play music and sing. And Aunt Eva says he was a big cut-up, could tell the funniest stories and do different voices and such. I wish I could have heard him."

Buddy looked at Katie with mock concern.

"He ain't been a part of your life much, has he? I'm sure I would have found a way, if I'd been lucky enough to have a girl like you." He put on his sad, downtrodden expression, but watched her face from the corner of his eye. "I'll never understand some people."

"Me neither." Katie said, staring off into space. "Auntie says my daddy's in bad health, but I don't know why he can't at least write to me. I used to write him letters, but I just quit."

"Well, don't you fret about it." Buddy patted her hand and then squeezed it, handing her the new nickel he'd recently carved a flower on. "You got me. I'd do anything for you that he would."

Katie smiled up at him and shook her head. "I'm a pretty lucky girl, I reckon. You beat all I ever seen."

Buddy had told Eva and Andrew, while he was sick, that he'd left things at the jungle in Gate City and needed to go get them. He'd been staying mostly in the shed at their place for months. Buddy knew it probably didn't make sense to them, why he would have something valuable to return for, and if he did, why he'd left it behind, but he was fortunate once again to have stumbled upon kind, generous people without suspicious natures.

Buddy certainly wasn't going to tell them or anyone else about the post office box in Gate City, the possibility of the check from the sale of his family's shack and some steep, rocky acres. That ship would someday come in, and when it did, he'd not have to live like a stray dog anymore. Every few weeks, he told the Nettles that he'd be gone for a couple of days, but assured them he'd be back.

"I'm going to go check on some things and visit my friend at the Mission," Buddy told them one morning, "Don't you worry, Andrew, I ain't running off on you. I'll be back to help you at the mill soon. I'll visit and rest at the Mission, eat a few good meals, and check in on the stories from the guys down there." He tipped his hat in Eva and Katie's direction.

Buddy set out then and walked a good ways before a fellow delivering some straw bales came along and let him ride part of the way on the wagon. When the wagon set him off down in the creek bend and he had to climb the long, steep climb of the Copper Creek Bluff, he had to stop and rest two more times. It worried him how weak he still was after his illness. By the time he got to the sad camp along the creek in Gate City, dusk had settled in. Most of the faces were new, but a few he remembered from an orchard he'd worked in for a while up in Wytheville. It didn't please him to see that the other familiar faces were Iron Mike, his crew, and that sad boy he kept with him, still there, Mike as silent and menacing as ever.

"Well, look what the cat dragged in," Iron Mike snarled, and he kept whittling on a piece of wood Buddy thought could be a knife handle.

Buddy ignored the man and headed toward the coffee pot sitting on the fire grate.

"Have some coffee, Buddy," Iron Mike snarled again. His bloodshot eyes and breath revealed the reason for his rude tone. He was clearly drunk.

Buddy turned around slowly and gave him a dead stare as he sipped the hot drink. He took another quick gulp and then sneered at Iron Mike. "I'd rather be what the cat dragged in than what he's coverin', Mike." The two young punks Mike was traveling with laughed before they could catch themselves. Mike's face darkened as though someone was choking him, and both boys stopped laughing, one turning deathly pale.

Iron Mike stood up and the air went still with tension. Buddy didn't react at all, but the men in the circle stood up or stepped back and looked at both men. Buddy still didn't move when Mike stepped toward him and kept walking until he was just inches away.

Mike whispered at him through gritted teeth. "Why don't you go off and find some fat Sunday School teacher or little school girl to climb on top of?"

In a split second, Buddy realized that Uncle Albert had been down at the Mission telling his tale. Buddy grinned at Iron Mike and leaned in even closer. He would have to be dealt with in due time. The men in the circle craned their necks so they could hear, but the wind kicked up and leaf rustle covered the words Buddy whispered into Iron Mike's ear. All anybody caught was the last word, "boy." With that, Buddy glanced over at Isaac, the frightened boy Iron Mike never let out of his sight. Buddy smirked, never looking back as he walked out of the circle of light in the direction of the creek.

After Buddy left the circle of men, Mike had whirled around, his face purple with rage. He swayed there a minute, turning up the bottle he carried in his pocket and then wiping his mouth with the back of his hand. Mike started off in the same direction as Buddy. The last anyone in the circle saw of them, they headed around the curve in the creek and out of sight, into the shadows.

No one thought anything of it when Mike didn't come back into camp. They figured he'd passed out somewhere and were glad of it. Isaac looked anxiously toward the dark woods where they'd disappeared, thinking that if Mike sobered up enough to walk back, there'd be bad times ahead for him that night. But there was no sign of Mike, and Isaac eventually drifted off to sleep, dreaming of sitting in church with his mom and grandma and of eating pie with them at a picnic.

When morning broke, the men were awakened by somebody hollering and a lot of commotion. Someone yelled again, telling them to come quick, and they all staggered to their feet and ran toward the voice. There, just about a hundred yards from where everyone had slept, Iron Mike lay half-in, half-out of the creek, his head bashed in, almost flat, the bottle in the soft marsh sand beside him. Buddy was nowhere in sight, and Isaac and his backpack had also disappeared. Nobody said a word, but they understood that the boy had finally had all he could take and had made his escape. The camp breathed a sigh of relief, and one of the men brought back a bottle of rotgut whiskey that night to celebrate.

The next morning, quite a few of them cleared out of the camp. As they left, several who were going in different directions decided to put warnings on the trees as they left. They drew what looked like a tic-tac-toe board turned slantwise: all the hobos in the area would know what that meant. *A crime was committed here. Not a safe place for a tramp.*

Eva noticed that Andrew treated her dislike of Buddy with amusement. He even seemed a little flattered by it—as though it were a testament to her liking her husband's personality better.

"You just don't like me listening to him at dinner instead of to you." He chuckled and pulled her close, kissing her neck gently all the way up to her chin. "And I know you love them chickens to death—anybody trying to steal your chicken ought not expect to be your best friend." He laughed louder.

Eva frowned, her mouth a straight line of irritation.

"You know you're my everything. Me and Buddy, we just enjoy talking. I promise, though, I'll start making more time for you."

"Drew, it isn't that." Eva suddenly felt so tired she almost shrugged and turned away. This was exhausting, this blindness. "Now he's trying to turn Katie against religion and going to church. You should have heard him the other day. He thought I was out back hanging out clothes, and they were on the front porch talking." She stopped and pressed her fingers against her forehead—she felt a headache brewing. "He told her him and his family stayed on their knees their whole life, either to his mean, drunk daddy or some rich lady his mother scrubbed floors for, that he sure wasn't getting down on his knees for God, who let so many bad things happen and played favorites like He did."

"I promise I'll talk to him." Andrew quickly gathered up his dinner and jacket and was out the door before Eva could say more. She sat down heavily in a chair and stared at the wall. *There are none so blind as he who will not see.*

That night at supper, Eva cooked up what she always called "Momma's supper." Boiled cabbage, turnips, potatoes, and a big skillet of cornbread. No meal was more delicious and comforting to her than this one. Growing up in a house with ten people around the table and no money had made this a common meal. She always remembered her momma scrubbing and slicing those little roots, adding lots of creamy butter and even a little honey sometimes to try to take away the sting, but of course, nothing could. Her momma would laugh and say, "It ain't no wonder they're shaped like a tear. They got some heat to 'em, don't they?"

As almost always, Buddy showed up for supper, shuffling in with his clothes still covered with sawdust, though he'd stopped outside the screen door and knocked off a few streaks. He was filthy and smelled bad, but Eva tried to overlook that. Hard work and sweaty smells were easier to take when they came from family or at least from people who loved you. Certainly, none of that was true with Buddy, and in fact, he wasn't even grateful or polite. He rarely even looked at Eva, much less talked to her or showed any appreciation for what she did for him. All he focused on was Andrew and Katie.

Buddy stopped and made an elaborate bow, pulling a big apple from his pocket. "Old man Dawson has the first Summer Rambos. Had to get one for my girl."

Katie smiled and put the apple beside her plate.

When Eva placed the food on the table and poured the men's coffee, she sat down and Katie asked the blessing. Buddy acted irritated that he had to stop talking to Andrew about the big job the twins were working on, but he did, and he slightly bowed his head but didn't close his eyes. As soon as Katie said "Amen," he reached for the potatoes, cabbage, and cornbread. Katie rushed to tell Eva about a book she was reading on Abigail Adams while Eva piled turnips on her plate and then handed the bowl to Buddy.

"No, I don't eat such. That's what trash and niggers eat." He shoveled the food into his mouth and didn't even look up when he said it.

Eva felt a stabbing pain in her head like someone had driven a railroad spike through it, and her face flamed hot. With no thought, but only a white rage, Eva jumped up, her chair clattering backward on the wood floor as she slammed her fork down on the table.

Andrew stared at her, his eyes as big as silver dollars.

Katie simply frowned and squinted, tilting her head to one side, watching Buddy.

"That's what we eat, me and my family, and all my people, *Mr.* Newman, and what you've been eating for free for months now, sitting with your feet under my table, eating my trashy food, Mr. Newman…"

By now, Buddy had pushed his chair back from the table, but he didn't stand. Instead he glared at her, dead on and unblinking, leaning forward in his chair as though he was going to rise, maybe strike her.

Andrew stood up, his eyes darting from Eva to Buddy. "Now, now, Eva..."

Buddy also stood, never breaking his locked gaze with Eva, and she didn't flinch or back away either, but instead took a step closer. At this point, Katie shifted her attention to Eva and watched. The little girl's eyes grew round with amazement.

"Fine. I won't stay where I'm not welcome." Buddy turned, picked his hat off the rack, and said quietly to Andrew, "I didn't know it was a crime to not like turnips." He smirked and ducked out the door.

"Lord, honey." Andrew shook his head and went back to his food.

It was more than Eva could handle. "Me? Are you serious, Drew? Don't you see how rude he is? How ungrateful?"

"That wasn't a nice thing to say, but I don't think he meant it, Auntie. I guess he's just tired," Katie said shyly.

Eva sat back down and put her head in her hands.

"This is something else. I can't believe you don't see how he's a troublemaker, how all he does is try to separate people." She looked at Andrew with a deep frown. "Don't you see he wants to separate us?" She pointed around the table. "You from Mac? Nancy Lawson from her family? It's all he does—make trouble and try to come between people." Eva stood up and moved to the sink, where she started washing the few dishes left from dinnertime.

Andrew and Katie sat in silence for a while, finishing their supper.

"I can't believe you're that upset over turnips." Katie shook her head and stared at the bowl that held them, but Eva didn't answer.

When they had finished eating, Katie started clearing the table and drying dishes for Eva.

"I'll be out in the barn," Andrew said, rising from the table and shutting the door quietly behind him as he left.

Eva only grew more hostile toward her husband's softness. The next morning after Katie left for school, she tried again to talk to Andrew. She said she didn't trust Buddy, said something was off about him. The more she thought about it, the more agitated she got. She wanted so badly to tell Andrew about the drawing, but she knew better. He'd say it wasn't Katie, that it was all her imagination, or just her resentment of Buddy. She wished she could have taken the drawing, yet for the first time it occurred to her to fear Buddy, how he might have retaliated.

"Drew, don't you see how he is? When he first come here, butter wouldn't melt in his mouth, bringing us all those gifts. Bringing me and Katie flowers and pictures, doing everything but lick your boots. But now, he's not even nice to me. He treats me like I'm some kind of servant in my own home."

Eva folded her arms and gave Andrew that stare he hated. Here was his wife asking him to get rid of one of his dearest friends, a favorite funny companion.

"Oh now, Eva, you're exaggerating. He's a single man, probably not the marrying kind. He don't have much experience with women, don't know how to act. His manners ain't the best, I'll have to say. But I think you're making too much of this." Andrew sighed deeply. "I'll talk to him, Eva, about appreciating what you do, and also about how he's got some money now and ought to cook some for himself, not show up here all the time for supper."

Eva was exasperated and sad, but she nodded. She really wanted Buddy out of their lives, and not just sometimes. Life had her like an old mule tethered to a plow, nothing in front of her but another rut.

"It'll all be fine, honey," Andrew said as he pecked her on the cheek before leaving for work.

Andrew decided to go on foot to the sawmill rather than saddle up his horse—walking always helped him think through a problem. There was no denying that Buddy had now gotten on Eva's last nerve; Andrew hoped encouraging Buddy to spend less time at the house would fix things. But there was no guarantee, and it was entirely possible Buddy would just take off completely, a possibility that made Andrew sad and anxious. All he could think of was how Buddy would shame him if he mentioned any of this. He might even bring it up to the guys at the sawmill, call Andrew "pussy-whipped" or say his wife rode him like a borrowed mule, or other such ridicule that the men use to belittle each other for weakness. Andrew remembered again, for the millionth time, the memory of his dad's shame at his inadequacies. Like most country boys, Andrew had to run the gauntlet of others' expectations. The various ways he had to prove himself to other males while growing up had become exhausting.

The imagined shaming at the sawmill brought a long-buried memory: his mind's eye had no trouble remembering hurt, so Andrew had no trouble remembering the ill-fated hunting trip, the heavy gun barrel wobbling in front of him, pointing at a deer. His father, two of Andrew's friends from school, and his Uncle Daniel were with him, spread out all through the laurel, watching. Deer always fed in that field, and the men knew they could let little Andy kill something there, at least a doe, if they just kept quiet. His dad's eyes sparkled as he whispered instructions. It was a long shot, but they'd practiced and practiced, Andrew learning how to steady the gun with his knee. He had squeezed the trigger just like his father taught him, but to his horror, it only clicked loudly. He hadn't put a bullet in the chamber! The deer, startled by the loud click, took off, tearing the brush as he went. The sad eyes of his father, the way the other men barely glanced at each other, the long walk back out of the woods emptyhanded—those things Andrew still remembered vividly. One of the many times his father had been disappointed.

23

After the confrontation with Eva regarding Buddy, Andrew mulled over the whole situation for days. He thought about the things Eva had told him, about the things Buddy had said to Katie, about showing the filthy pictures on those coins to the Dockery twins.

Putting all that together with the visit from the church women who came to see Eva and complain about Buddy's lack of morals was a final wake-up call for Andrew. *Those busy-bodies have got their nerve, but they've also got a point.* He decided that Buddy Newman needed to know what everyone in town knew, the gossip and the doubts about him, and most of all, how his actions could affect Andrew and his family and his business.

That evening, when everyone else had gone home from the mill, Buddy came into the little shed, sat down, and propped his feet up on another chair.

"I feel like forty miles of bad road. But we got a lot done today."

Andrew nodded. They sat in silence for a moment, and Buddy shifted uneasily, glancing at Andrew.

"Buddy, everybody in town knows about you and Nancy on the river-bank."

"What? Who knows? Surely, nobody ain't listening to that loudmouth drunk…"

"For heaven's sake, Buddy, out on the ground in broad daylight? With poor old Nancy? What were you thinking?"

Buddy jumped up and threw his hat on the floor, his eyes wild and darting. "What do you expect me to do? I ain't got no wife, ain't no man like me got no wife to wait on him at home or do nothin' else for him. Them holier-than-thou holy-rollers need to get off their high horses and shut their hypocrite mouths about me. I ain't…"

"Buddy, listen to me." Andrew spoke quietly, keeping his stare steady and not at all friendly. "I can't tell you how to live, don't care what you do in your off time long as it don't affect me and mine. But I got news for you, Buddy. Most people do that kind of thing in private, at night, or behind closed doors."

Buddy dropped his eyes and slowly sat down. He looked back at Andrew with big tears in his eyes. "All right, Andrew, you're right. I ought not done it, but she begged me. Said she was tired of being alone and not knowing what other women knew, not having what other women had. She begged me to, right then."

At that moment, something crackled behind Andrew's eyes. The air felt as though lightning had struck somewhere close. Buddy Newman was lying, and Andrew knew it. Nancy Lawson was as prim and proper and shy a lady as he'd ever met. She could be found at church almost every time it opened, cooked for every family that had a death, and was as polite and proper a lady as his own mother, though with a stronger country accent and demeanor. No, she didn't beg to be in this story. He just knew that wasn't how it was, that the tears weren't shame or embarrassment or regret or remorse. They were fake. For the first time, it occurred to Andrew that Buddy really might not be who he claimed.

24

After the encounter with Aunt Becky, the boys lost interest in the haunted house inside the tangled yard on the back road. Henry was nothing to be scared of, just a crazy old sick man who'd killed his brother. But Katie, more interested than ever, was able to convince Alice to join her in her Mission. The little girl was obsessed with the idea that she and Alice should try to help them, as Aunt Becky said, "Do something pleasing to the Lord." She swore Alice to secrecy and hatched an elaborate plan to get inside the house to talk with Mary.

One warm day, both girls told their parents they were going to a revival at the little Baptist church at the end of the road, but they would be a little late because they were going to go across the ridge and walk Sally Peterson to church with them. They had already put together a little gift basket and hid it in an outbuilding: it had some eggs, a testament the missionary ladies had brought to school, a piece of needlework Alice had made, and one of Eva's bird drawings. The girls were pleased with themselves and their plan and excited that evening as they started off toward the house.

"Now, what exactly are you going to say when you go to the door?" Alice frowned.

"I'm going to say we just wanted to drop by to check on them in Christian love and could we come in and visit a spell."

Alice looked skeptical, but nodded.

"I think they'll be glad to see us." Katie smiled at the thought. "People don't stop to see them because they're scary. But I'm not scared. They need our help—I just know it. And there's some reason I'm supposed to go there."

When the girls reached the house, they stopped, listened, and watched the windows, hoping someone would peek out.

"Are you gonna go knock? I'm not." Alice folded her arms, and Katie gave her a withering look.

"OK, fine." Katie took the basket from Alice and marched right up onto the porch. She hesitated only a second and then knocked loudly.

It seemed like hours passed until the door opened a crack and a watery eye appeared. A foul odor also escaped the crack, and Katie instinctively backed away, covering her face with one hand. Her plan on what to say fled, her mind as blank as a cat's.

"Who are you?" The voice sounded strange, as though from someone with a bad sore throat and marbles in her mouth.

"I'm... I'm Katie Teague, ma'am, Ezra and Alma Teague's daughter. I live just down the road with my aunt. May... could my friend Alice and I come in? We brought you something."

The eye didn't move, didn't blink or retreat. Night had begun to fall, and the silence was beautiful, the breeze sweet as honey. Just then, something made a loud cracking sound in the woods to one side of the house, and Katie felt the hair on the back of her neck rise. *Is that him? Is that Henry?* Katie looked back at Alice, who was staring into the woods, too.

The door cracked open wider, and an aging hand reached out and took the basket. The strange, muffled voice said, "Thank ye. Mighty kind." The door started to slowly shut again.

"Uh, wait, please! I'd love to visit a while." But the door had already shut. The musty air from the house that smelled like a dirt cellar, like a fresh-turned grave, puffed into Katie's face as the faint shuffling faded away inside.

25

Advice

I was sitting by the window fretting today, wearing myself out thinking the same thoughts, the same sentences, seeing the same scenes over and over and over in my head until I thought I would scream. None of this is helping matters one bit.

I happened to look down at my hands, and it startled me. I don't know how I hadn't noticed it. I knew I looked like Momma. Everybody has always said that. Today though it was like I was her looking down at my hands. It was just an unnerving experience. They ache in cold and fatigue the way hers did, the skin is wrinkled and papery, every vein dark blue and swollen. It's so strange, though, that even though I look just like her, more than any of her other children, I'm Daddy's child through and through. I have my mother's bones only, my father's moods and restlessness.

My mother would be the one I'd so love to talk to about Katie, about what to do with her, about how I should handle this situation with Buddy Newman. On second thought, maybe not. I know Momma well enough to know she'd never put up with someone she didn't trust and who had drawn a picture of a naked child. But then Momma would have never understood Andrew, about his loneliness and his need for friends. Maybe it's best she isn't here.

Discovery

I haven't slept much at all the last two nights. I don't know what in the world I'm going to do. That drawing I found is there every time I close my eyes to try to sleep. All I see is not just the drawing, but the image of him making the drawing, rubbing his thumb along lines of Katie's body to soften and shape the lines, his breath going in and out, as he fantasized over every inch of the beautiful child in the drawing.

I do know about how you feel about things you draw. There is such love and connection. It is planted deep in your mind—you can see whatever it is as plain when you close your eyes as if it was right there in front of you. That's what makes you able to draw it like that—the seeing and the loving. Maybe it's a woman he's been with, maybe even a wife he left behind. Maybe he doesn't think about Katie that way. I can pray that. But I can't convince myself. And I don't know what in the world to do.

I was so shocked by it that I never gave a second's thought about stealing it and showing it to Andrew. I have no proof now it even exists, and I know Buddy Newman would just deny it, call me crazy probably.

Rage

If I don't get this off my chest to somebody, I'm probably going to explode. They'll find a pile of ashes where I'm sitting. Buddy Newman has done broke his plate with me. I want him gone from my house and my life so much. I just see more and more that he ain't nothing but a troublemaker. He has caused nothing but trouble and worry since he got here, and he's nobody's "Buddy," no matter what he says.

Here I've been cooking and washing his dishes for months now and all he's done is cut us some firewood a few times. Of course, he is a big help down at the mill, and I know that means a lot to Andrew, but it still don't make up for all the food he's eat or the trouble he's caused.

The other night he turned his nose up at my cooking, which it's fine if somebody doesn't like something once in a while. I can't eat chicken livers, for example. I just don't like them at all, and the texture literally makes me gag. But even so, I'd never say anything insulting about eating them. Who does that? I'll tell you who—Buddy Newman.

When I offered him cooked turnips the other night, he shoved them away and said only white trash and niggers eat that. I couldn't believe it. Country people eat whatever they can get, no matter what it is and no matter what color they are. They ain't no shame in being poor. I just wanted to grab him by the raggedy coat and throw his sorry behind out in the yard. My momma loved turnips and fixed them twice a week, and the idea that some hobo walking around in shoes with soles so thin you could read the newspaper through them would look down his nose at my momma and us, think he's too good for us, it just made my blood boil. And of course, he just giggled about it, thought it was a big joke. I'm starting to despise him.

Scared

I am almost afraid to write this here. If anyone ever found it, that would be bad. But it's more than that. To write it is to make it true and real. But if I don't say it somewhere, I may burst like a summer pear on the ground too long. When I went to the store today, there was a gang of people standing and talking off to the side. It was a mixed group of women and old men, and they looked glum and tense, like they were uneasy and didn't know what to do with themselves. I spoke to everyone and tried to start up a conversation, but they all acted funny. It was obvious something was bad wrong.

I went up to Maggie Williams and she started telling me what was causing the commotion. Turns out they'd found Uncle Albert Smith dead. He was down along the river where he stayed a lot of the time. His head was kind of in the edge of the water. It looked like he slipped and hit his head on a rock. There was a whiskey bottle next to him, and a bundle of clothes and a fishing pole was nearby. Now, people probably ain't surprised at all, won't even bat an eye. He was often staggering drunk and it's certainly not hard to imagine him being too drunk to fish, as sad as that sounds, way too drunk to navigate walking on slippery rocks out to the deeper part of his fishing hole.

But what bothers me about it is this: ain't it awful convenient that after walking across those rocks drunk and sober for his many years—probably 60 plus—that he falls and kills hisself just in time to stop him telling stories about Buddy Newman? Mighty handy, ain't it?

Here's the real shocker: it comes just two days after Katie come in telling that RJ said that Nancy Lawson had up and disappeared. Said he heard his momma, who is Nancy's cousin, telling some folks that they hadn't heard from or seen her for a while and went up to check on her. They found a note in a sealed envelope nailed to the door. It was addressed to Anna Lee or David Lane—RJ's mother and uncle. It was a letter from Nancy saying she was going up to eastern Kentucky to stay with her daddy's people and make a new start.

Anna Lee said it was strange that she's made the mistake of saying it was her daddy's people that lived in Kentucky when in fact it was her mother's, but Anna Lee said she hadn't been at all herself since all that happened with Buddy. Now ain't that another happy little break for our buddy, Mr. Buddy? I can't stop thinking about all of it. I just have a sick feeling about it. I know it's probably crazy, but I can't help it. I hear alarms going off in my head that sound like a church bell ringing and ringing. I done made up my mind. I'm going to go steal that drawing and show it to Andrew. I'm tired of worrying about this. If I'm wrong, well, it wasn't like I had malicious reasons. Either way, Buddy Newman can move on down the road and go on with his life.

Life and Love

I smiled at the title I put on this—it's not like you can talk about those two things in a few minutes in your diary, can you? Life is really just two things—time and love—that's what it all comes down to. It came to me as I've been spending all my time lately worrying and fretting and thinking of everything negative, that I need to rethink my perspective a little bit and be more grateful! I have been here before. I thought when I was younger and everything in my life had fallen apart and I'd lost everyone and everything that mattered—my momma and daddy, my husband, my baby—that life was over, there can't be nothing after that.

Then Drew showed up and suddenly life was back, time was back. And then we moved here. Now, where my mommy and daddy lived, no matter what they did, how hard they worked at it, it wasn't pretty like this place is. It was always overgrown and ragged, too many cedars and briers, too much mud. But now, with Drew in my life, I live where it's clean and green, where I watch does and their fawns out in the field, hawks flashing in the sky.

Everything about it is just perfect, like a painting, and for some reason, everywhere I look I'm reminded of something in the Bible. There's a huge, top-heavy oak tree out in the middle of the pasture all by itself. In my head I call it the Tree of Life.

I watched Drew cutting firewood the other day across the far pasture. He had his shirt off and he swung the ax, raised and lowered it over and over, and it was like a dance, and I felt such a rush of love that I wanted to go over there and put my arms around him and kiss and kiss his whole face. He is such a good, good man. I heard the words of the prophet Micah: "He has showed you, O man, what is good; and what does the Lord require of you but to do justice, and to love kindness, and to walk humbly with your God." I can't explain all I felt at that moment, but to know that he works as hard as he does every day just for me and Katie, that he's changed his whole life to give mine back to me, fills me with something I can't even give breath to.

The clock in Mary's house was the heartbeat in her world and her connection with reality. Henry lay like a baby, babbling occasionally, sometimes looking at her for a second with his full mind and heart engaged, and seemed to know who she was. Mostly, though, he slept.

Sometimes when he seemed deep in his dreams, she would go out and walk a little ways through the woods, savoring each season's magic. In spring she looked for morel mushrooms, Jack-in-the-pulpit, wild daffodils left over from some old homestead long since burned or torn down. In winter she'd have a chance to study the rock ledges hidden in warmer weather by the canopy of green, the shapes that ice could take as it remade itself every few days.

She'd lost track of how long she'd been there in that house. Her mind and her memories were scrambled now. She'd been living as normal and peaceful a life as you could possibly live in as normal and peaceful a family as anyone could be born into until the day she heard about Henry. She had always been sweet on him, but had told no one in the world—not her mother, not her best girlfriends, not even her sisters. They wouldn't have understood in the first place, when they all were young, and they certainly didn't understand after Henry did what he did.

Mary didn't invite any of them to the wedding they'd hastily arranged in the front room of the house a few months after she moved in to take care of Henry when he got out of the mental hospital. Mary had called a couple of neighbors over to serve as witnesses. There were no flowers and no ring until Mary went upstairs and found a little pearl ring in a box that belonged to Henry's mother. The preacher pronounced them man and wife and told Henry he could kiss his bride, but he just stood there with that blank stare, so Mary kissed him on the cheek. Her little dog barked and Mary whirled around and said, "Hush, Feist! Right now!" and he did. Everyone hugged them and left and that was it. No one had ever been invited in since then.

There were many tall tales about Henry: that he killed his brother and boiled him and ate him, that he tortured animals on their farm, that he skinned rats alive and tacked their hides on the barn wall. All that was a lie. He had killed his brother, he said, because he had no choice. Claude had slapped off his glasses with an open hand in front of a neighbor woman who was visiting. "He crossed a line," Henry had said, and then he calmly accepted his punishment.

Everyone had been very shocked by Mary's behavior, and people from both families, as well as some neighbors and friends and fellow church members, tried to convince her to come home and let Henry go his own way. Mary couldn't really answer them when they asked her why, except to say, "But I've always known this was supposed to happen." People eventually started saying what many were thinking. "Mary is as crazy as he is. Who would have thought that?"

Getting out and walking was the only thing that kept her sane all these years. It was on one of these jaunts that she noticed something she didn't like, a man she didn't yet know, who seemed to be following the children. A man with dark, curly hair and the shoulders of an ox. She knew about those kids coming by the place all the time. She'd seen them out in the road, pointing up at the house and jabbering among themselves or just standing and staring, imagining. It bothered her some days; on others, it just made her smile.

They would leave her disturbing notes that were also so funny she had to laugh.

Are you witches? You got haints in that house? It looks like it. RJ wants to know. Please write us back. —Alice Lane

She had seen her and Henry's lifelong friend, Aunt Becky Cain, talking to them out in the road one day, and she wished so much at that moment that she could open the door and invite Becky in so they could talk and talk for hours, their voices carrying them back across the years to the people they once were. Becky might be the one person in the world who wouldn't judge her or Henry or the way they lived, but Mary knew better than to chance it. *People ain't nothing but trouble. Ain't no need of starting something.*

On that other day after the kids went on down the road, she saw the dark-haired stranger showing too much interest in what they were doing. She'd noticed the tall man come along about five minutes later. She didn't think much of it at the time. Men she didn't know were always walking by. The trains brought them in here from everywhere— lost souls, desperate souls, the hungry, the hurting, the scared. A whole world of families existed who had no idea where their sons, fathers, or brothers had gone, out in the world desperately trying to find a way to eat, to make a little money they might send back home to relatives they might never see again.

But then it happened a second time. Last Sunday, the two girls came by themselves. Mary wondered what happened to the boys, why these girls took it upon themselves to try to come into her world. The girls climbed up on the porch and actually knocked. Mary stood back in the shadows where they couldn't see her. They were carrying a little basket again.

They'd also come the week before, bringing the first basket full of wonderful things. She'd marveled at them, picked up the drawings and embroidery again and again. Children were a wonder sometimes, how different they were from grownups, how much closer to God and the heavens. But she didn't want to encourage them, as much as she almost wanted to. It was in their best interests not to hang around there. Some kind of trouble would come from it.

As she'd watched them on the second visit, the girls had both seemed startled, looking over to their right toward the tangled brush at the edge of the yard. After a minute, they turned their attention back to the door. Mary had stood still as a mouse. The girls finally turned and went back down the broken stone steps with a dejected expression on their faces. They stopped and looked back at the house one more time and chatted for just a minute. Relieved to see them finally move on down the road toward the church, Mary had started to turn away from the window to check on Henry when she saw a flicker of motion out of the corner of her eye. It was that same man! He stepped out of the brush at the edge of the yard and stood there for a minute, but then he seemed to think better of it. He slipped back into the brush and disappeared. Mary assumed he went on back up the road in the direction the girls had come from.

She suddenly realized it was no coincidence that she'd seen him twice. He was following the girls! Mary felt sick to her stomach. She'd heard about men like this. *Surely there's something I can do.*

The next time Mary saw the girls come down the road, she followed them but stayed out in the woods, parallel to the road. They turned out at Mt. Pleasant Church and went to the swimming hole on Copper Creek that everyone called "the foam hole" because of a swirling eddy of frothy water that circled in a little bend in the creek. Anyone on the high ridge above could see it clearly, but those in the creek or near it couldn't see the onlooker unless they looked carefully. The girls had on boys' pants and shirts, and they jumped into the creek from a big rock jutting out from the little waterfall on the far side. They squealed and laughed and talked excitedly, but Mary couldn't make out what they were saying.

She positioned herself on the far side of a big oak that shielded her from the girls if they happened to look up. Just a couple of feet to her left, a sheer rock cliff rose at least one hundred feet above the creek. Anyone approaching would have to come the same way she had, or else along the creek far below, but also from the right and then up the creek on the neighbor's property. The girls had been playing awhile when she caught a glimpse of movement—sure enough, it came from her right, down along the creek. Someone must have walked in from the neighboring farm and stood behind a thicket of laurel. Mary could see him clearly, but he had to be invisible to the girls. It was that man, the same one who'd followed them the day they knocked on her door! Mary felt sick and cold, and a shiver ran down her arms as they turned to goose flesh. *Peter said the devil prowls like a roaring lion, seeking someone to devour.*

When the girls got out of the water, they climbed up on one of the big rocks to dry off, chattering and laughing. The man turned then and slipped away silently. Mary followed him back out to the top of the ridge and watched until he was out of sight.

Later at home, Mary sat in her rocking chair and replayed the scene by the creek in her mind. She knew if she'd had a chance to talk to the sheriff, or if she'd gone and knocked on the Nettles' door and said, "A hobo is following Katie and may do her harm," the odds of anyone believing her were slim. So she did what she'd always done. She talked to someone she was sure would listen and take care of it all. In her rocking chair by the window, she prayed out loud:

"Dear Lord, I come to You as always with thanks and praise for all You do for us. I also need Your help, Lord, like never before. I think there's a bad man nearby who means to do harm, and You're the only One who can stop it. I'm going to lay it in Your hands and know that You'll protect the little girl. You just let me know if there's anything I need to do to help. In Jesus' name, Amen."

27

Mac stuck with Andrew through thick and thin. Even when Andrew was doing something as unpopular as chasing Ezra Teague, Mac had stuck by him. Despite their great differences in background, temperament, and social class, they trusted each other implicitly. Mac knew Andrew was the best sort of man and a hard worker, so he'd committed to helping Andrew and Eva realize their dreams.

Despite being willing to do almost anything for Andrew, it was becoming more and more apparent to him that putting up with the likes of Buddy Newman was just too much. Not only did Buddy have a questionable character and morals, but he also was nothing but a troublemaker. Mac had never seen anything like it.

Buddy would take the Dockery brothers off one at a time and try to find a way to trigger their natural jealousy and competitiveness with each other, telling each one privately how Andrew had bragged on him and was thinking about giving him a big bonus on his next job, except that his brother was holding him back. Andrew had done no such thing, of course, and the childishness of the game Buddy played astonished Mac.

But it wasn't just schoolyard pranks with Buddy. He seriously worked to cause trouble between people, even between the other workers and Mac, and worst of all, between Mac and Andrew.

They were taking a break in the shade, waiting for some wood to be loaded out before they went back to sawing. Buddy whittled on one of his little birds, and Mac was lost in thought. Buddy handed the little bird over to him. "What do you think?"

Mac gave the bird a passing glance and said, "Looks like it might fly off." He was in no mood to pay Buddy any compliments. He said as little to him as he could get by with.

"That's what Andrew and Katie say." He chuckled to himself. "Eva don't say much about it, though. She's jealous, I think." Buddy grinned over at Mac and nodded. "She ain't never liked me too good since she seen how I could draw and stuff. She likes to do that, too, you know, so I think she's jealous. Women are like that."

"Eva has always been down to earth and humble. And she's kind as she can be to everybody, especially you." Mac gave Buddy a dead-level stare and then turned and poured out the rest of his coffee.

"Well, yes, she's been good to me, but she's jealous as she can be, doesn't like to see how good I can draw, doesn't like to see how Katie and Andrew like me and sit and talk to me. She's just like a little young'un." He stopped talking and studied Mac's face, but Mac returned his gaze without comment. "I guarantee she's stuck her nose in my business just for spite, or Andrew wouldn't ever have said nothin' to me about Uncle Albert or none of that." Buddy's face was turning red, and when Mac laughed out loud, the hobo's eyes narrowed to a razor's edge of rage. It tickled Mac to death that Buddy had apparently slipped up and revealed something undesirable.

"Good for her!" Mac laughed again. "You got called out for acting like trash and bringin' a good woman down to your level, did you?" He gave Buddy that same dead-level I-dare-you stare again. "I think it's pretty funny."

A few days later, Mac went to the big wooden toolbox he kept in one of the sheds. He was searching for something to fix a belt that had come off the conveyor, and when he raised the lid, a copperhead almost as big as his wrist raised its head. He cried out and jumped back. After he had a second to gather his thoughts, it occurred to him there was no way the snake got in there by itself. He was sure Buddy had done it, and he went to Andrew and told him so.

"What are the chances, Drew? We've been working here for years now, and I ain't never seen a snake crawl up under that lid, have you?"

Andrew gave Mac a puzzled stare. "What are you saying, Mac? That somebody put it in there trying to kill you? That's a pretty crazy accusation."

"Maybe," said Mac, "but all I know is that I laughed at Buddy for complaining about something, and then a few days later this happens." Mac decided to keep it to himself that Buddy had been complaining about Eva.

"I swear, you and Eva are just hung up on poor old Buddy. Look, I know he's difficult and can try anybody's patience, but all this"—Andrew gestured toward Mac—"just seems crazy to me, to be honest. I don't think he's anything like you and Eva claim. He ain't no lunatic."

Mac felt a wave of frustration and fatigue wash over him. He wasn't sure what he'd do, but he wasn't the sort of fellow to make a hasty decision about anything.

"OK, Drew. OK." Mac turned to leave the office. He glanced back once, and Andrew was staring after him with a puzzled look.

So far, Mac hadn't quit a thing in his life. He seldom had trouble getting along with people, and it was a rare day that he lost his temper. He was a calm little stream that almost always went with the flow. But for the first time in his life, he was about ready to walk away from something that mattered: Andrew and the mill. He decided he'd help him get the jobs out they'd contracted for recently, but before he let Andrew say "yes" to another one, he meant to tell him. *You don't stay on the wagon with the runaway horse until it runs off a cliff. You get out soon as you can. When something can't be saved, you don't have to go down with it.*

28

Andrew stepped out onto the porch with his morning coffee as quietly as he could, holding the screen door so it wouldn't slam shut and wake Eva or Katie. The sun still hid behind the ridge, the morning air silky and cool on his face. He found himself out here before dawn most mornings now, after restless nights of tossing and turning. His mind and nerves were starting to fray. It was an exhausting burden, this secret he kept to himself, but he couldn't tell Eva—at least not yet—that he was in real financial trouble.

His growing realization that Eva and Mac were right about Buddy weighed heavily on his chest, too, as though something was sitting on him and he couldn't draw a full, deep breath. He had to admit it: when Eva told him about Uncle Albert being found dead in the river, his head smashed, it had rattled him to the core. Of course, nobody in town thought much of it. They hated to hear the news, but people just shook their heads and said, "Poor ol' Uncle Albert. It's a wonder it didn't happen sooner." They naturally blamed the drinking, and maybe his age. Andrew hadn't heard of a single person who suspected foul play.

As Andrew sipped his coffee and watched a sliver of orange light line the ridge, he couldn't help but have the same thought as Eva: it was an interesting coincidence that somebody Buddy hated, and who had something on him, suddenly turned up dead. But then it came to him again, as it often did—the nights of storytelling and laughing their heads off, Buddy revealing his grief over his hard childhood with big tears in his eyes—and he tried to reassure himself that his suspicions were completely crazy.

Andrew had seen another disturbing item in the newspaper, but he hadn't even mentioned it to Eva. There had been a murder down in the hobo camp in Gate City. They found a body down there, a man who appeared to have been in a bad fight or beaten to death. The killing had occurred when Buddy stayed down there for a few days. These dark thoughts swirled, mixing with worry about money and the mill, so that the breathtaking pink-fingered dawn opening before him failed to bring its usual peace and comfort.

He was slowly coming to accept the idea that Buddy needed to move on. Even if he wasn't a dangerous person, and even if Andrew and Eva were letting their imaginations run away with them, there was no denying that Mac was right: the character of the sawmill had completely changed. Everyone still worked fairly well together, and to an outsider, nothing might seem off at all. But Andrew could easily see that now there was mostly silence and tension any man could cut with a knife; it was rarely interrupted unless someone exploded in anger or made a sarcastic remark to someone else. He was sure Mac and the Dockery twins felt it, too.

Restoring the good feeling of the mill would not be easy. Neighbors Joe and John McClellan had once had a horse die in the edge of a pond on the back forty acres of their farm and hadn't found it for quite a while. A long time had passed before the smell cleared and the pond could be used again. Though Andrew couldn't bring himself to blame it all on Buddy, it would be a long time before the mill recovered from his time there.

Andrew had also become aware of some little things at home that he hadn't noticed before. Buddy often tried to step in and do things for Katie rather than let Andrew or Eva take care of her needs. Whether helping her with a difficult homework assignment, answering a question about anything and everything under the sun, or teaching her little songs, Buddy jumped in first, oftentimes not even giving Andrew a chance. It seemed he not only wanted as much of Katie's attention as he could get, but he also wanted to undermine everyone else, as if Eva and Andrew were inferior to him in some way.

The rooster crowed, and Andrew knew Eva would soon be up to start breakfast. He took one last sip of the coffee and tried to push these heavy thoughts away. Buddy was occupying way too much of his heart and mind, and with the financial troubles he faced, he hadn't the time or energy for it. But the thought of Buddy going away, going out of their lives, filled Andrew with the old sadness that used to be his constant companion.

29

With the magical days of summer winding down, it was time for the annual homecoming at church, and the women of Wayland Baptist Church were in high gear. Some had been saving bits of cornbread and old biscuits for several days so they could make dressing to go with the chicken. Others had sweated stains on their housedresses gathering berries or apples to make pies. Eva had picked, strung, and broken enough green beans to fill up a washtub, it seemed to her, and she was up at daylight, shiny pieces of fatback floating in the rising steam. She had cornbread in the oven, and two apples pies she'd made the day before tempted her from the pie cabinet. Today was going to be fun.

After the service, Rev. Neeley asked the blessing, and the young boys made a break for the tables of food, nearly knocking each other down as they competed for the first spot in line. People were laughing and talking and hugging. Eva loved these rare moments when so many could be together like this, away from their animals, the monotony of the work, and the stress of the times. There was much to worry about and pray for, and they were so happy to be together to do it, to be reminded of how many were just like them, and to take comfort in that.

Eva was uncovering her pies and putting spoons into the bowls of every delicious thing imaginable when Edith Barnes showed up at her side. Eva always dreaded Edith catching up with her at these things—not that Edith was a bad person, but she was just "too mouthy," as her daddy would have put it. She talked a mile a minute and oftentimes said things that shocked her listener. She didn't seem to have any sense of gossip or when she needed to keep things to herself. She once cornered Eva after prayer meeting with a running monologue about the problem she was having with hemorrhoids, and Eva thought she'd die of embarrassment before she got away from the woman.

"Hey, dear, how you doing?" Edith put a pot of dumplings on the table and wiped the sweat off her forehead with a dingy little piece of cloth, probably once a handkerchief, which she then tucked down into her bosom. "I'm about to roast."

"Doing just fine, Edith. How 'bout yourself?"

"Oh, pretty good, pretty good. Can't complain, nobody cares." She pulled at each side of her dress and looked down to see that it was smooth and buttoned up after returning the handkerchief to its shelf. "Say, is that tramp who was working for your husband still around? I can't remember his name."

"Well, yes, why?" Eva regretted saying it as soon as it popped out of her mouth. She knew she should have just pretended she didn't hear Edith, just turned away or lied or anything other than invite Edith to talk more, here in the churchyard where the ground had ears.

"Well, I need to tell you something for your own good." She took Eva by the arm long enough to steer her away from the table, off to an empty corner. "I talked to Nancy Lawson since she's come back."

Eva managed to stop herself from crying out, "Oh, thank God!" Edith would have been puzzled, and Eva certainly couldn't tell her she'd feared that Nancy was dead, possibly killed by the insane hobo. "Well, that's good news. I hate to see anybody forced away from the place they love."

Edith leaned in closer to Eva and cleared her throat. She lowered her voice to such a whisper that Eva had to watch her lips to know what she was saying. "She said what happened out there on the river wasn't her idea." Edith turned and looked over her shoulder, as if idly watching the crowd during a lull in the conversation. "He gave her liquor, she told me, when she'd never drunk in her life. Put it in some apple cider he said he bought from the ladies at the Mission in Gate City. Then he forced himself on her, even when she told him to stop. You know it's true, Eva. You just know it. Nancy would never do something like that."

Something lurched in Eva's stomach, and she could hardly breathe. Buddy hadn't taken advantage of a lonely spinster and sweet-talked her into a wild love affair. That wasn't what happened here. Eva suddenly felt more than short of breath; she was dizzy and lightheaded.

"I have to go sit with my family, Edith. Thank you for telling me. I'm glad Nancy is back home." She inched her way toward the table where Andrew and Katie were sitting. Eva's knees felt rubbery, and the sunlight streaking the floor broke into odd angles of color. She sank into a chair next to her husband and tried to focus on the delicious food in front of her, the smiling faces of dear friends and neighbors. But her mind was elsewhere, obsessed with a plan to steal that drawing from Buddy.

30

Eva was hanging clothes out on the line when she heard it—the sound of a horse running as hard as possible, with a wagon behind. She dropped the clothes in the basket and ran for the back door to get her gun. Nobody would be running that hard unless they were scared or hurt, or the animal had spooked and was running away with them.

She rounded the corner of the house to see Jesse Davidson standing up in a wagon with a couple of lathered horses straining at the bits, wild-eyed and breathing heavily.

"Eva! Eva Nettles!" he called to her as he pulled at the reins, trying to settle the team.

"What in the world, Jesse! What's wrong?"

"It's the bank, the bank in Fort Blackmore, the one in Dungannon, too, I think. Maybe all of them. They're closing, going under, Eva. If you have any money in there, you better go get it. I saved three hundred in the bank in Fort Blackmore, what I was going to build my house with."

"Wait… what?" Eva tried to process what she was hearing. "Where is our money? How can they do that?"

"Nobody ain't got any money. I don't understand it. And you got to pay interest and so forth or the bank goes bankrupt. They ain't got no money to loan. That's what Doc McConnell explained to me."

There was no time to try to understand. Eva turned and ran to the barn without another word. She'd have to hurry and get back before school let out. If she lost all that money, she didn't know what she'd do, but one thing for sure: she'd never tell Andrew. He'd be better off not knowing.

She hitched up her own team and buggy and whipped the horses until she was ashamed of herself, all the way to Fort Blackmore, standing up because she feared the springboard seat would hit a big bump going over the mountain and throw her to the ground. When she pulled into the one main street in Fort Blackmore, a crowd had gathered in front of the small bank building as if waiting for something; there were two boards nailed across the door in the shape of an X. A sign read, *Closed until further notice.*

A cry came from her throat, and Eva thought for a moment it was someone else. She jumped down and pushed through the crowd. They looked around at one another and finally Joseph McConnell said, "Miz Nettles, they say our money is gone. It ain't in there no more. Just gone."

Eva nodded, mumbled her thanks, and somehow walked back to the wagon, feeling as if she were floating, as if her head might drift up into the sky like one of those balloons she'd seen floating over Paris in magazine pictures.

She climbed back up on the wagon and headed toward home. When she was well out of town, Eva pulled off the road into a little wayside by a cornfield and sobbed. Her uncle had promised to sell her some land that joined theirs on the back side of their farm. Some was good pasture land, some good for timber. He'd watched her grow up and admired her talent with a pencil and paper. With no children of his own, he'd unofficially adopted Eva and her family. He'd asked for one thousand dollars for the whole parcel whenever she could get it together. Eva had been almost there—$981.47, the last statement said.

She'd worked, daydreamed, and schemed for four years. She'd been determined to do it all by herself, to be able to feel she'd really accomplished something in her life besides cooking and cleaning, sewing and ironing. She'd kept it a secret from Andrew. All those hours stitching on beautiful quilts, all the extra eggs carted to Blair's Store, the drawings of people's children and grandchildren for Christmas, the ginseng she'd found and sold. All gone. And why? How could such a thing happen?

When Andrew came in for dinner, he wondered why the kitchen was empty, no sign of food or Eva. A muffled sound came from the bedroom. When he walked over and peered into the room, there she lay on the bed, her eyes swollen and red.

"Honey, what in the world is wrong?"

Eva sat up slowly. Andrew's heart pounded with the fear that she was going to tell him someone died, that she was sick, that something awful had happened. Eva wasn't a woman to cry or sulk—something had to be terribly wrong.

"I have to tell you something, Andrew, something I should have told you from the start." She patted the bed beside her. When he sat down and took her hand, she told him all about the money she'd been squirreling away for years, about the land she'd planned to buy, and about the bank closing that morning. "When I got there, there were two boards like this—" she crossed her hands into an X—"and they said everybody's money is gone."

"Oh my God, I can't believe this." Andrew rose abruptly, walking out of the room and into the kitchen to start a pot of coffee. It was all he could think to do.

"Come in here, Eva. I have something I have to tell you, too."

When Eva came to the kitchen, dabbing at her swollen eyes, Andrew had already sat down at the table, resting his head on his arms.

"If only I'd known." He lifted his head and looked at her with tear-filled eyes. "If only you'd told me, talked to me about it. Why didn't you, Eva?"

"I… I wanted to do something all by myself, something you'd be proud of. I know that might sound crazy to you, Andrew. But I never done nothing in my life but take care of people who couldn't take care of themselves. I've worked like a dog, but it ain't like I got anything to show for it. This was something I did mostly with my talent for making things and such." Andrew reached out and cupped her small hands in his big rough ones.

"I can understand that, I can. And it's a better excuse than mine."

"What do you mean?"

"If I'd known you had that much money, Eva, I would have used it to make payments on the mill." He stood up, poured coffee for each of them, and then looked out the window so he couldn't see her reaction. "We're behind on payments. I didn't want to tell you, thinking it would surely pick up down there. I couldn't stand the thought of worrying you, or even worse, I couldn't stand the thought of you thinking I was a failure. My hiding something this big from you wasn't right, and it's nothing but my puffed-up pride. At least you were just trying to help us out, better us. And by using your talents."

"Andrew, I know it's not your fault. You've worked like a dog down there." Eva rose and stepped behind him, hugging his waist. "Surely it'll pick up soon."

"No, I don't think so. It's not what I'm hearing." He turned and pulled her close, patting her hair as if soothing a child. "I'm so sorry, honey, about the land. I know you really wanted it, and you worked so hard." He took her by the hand. "Let's sit down here at the table and work us out a plan. We'll just have pie and coffee for dinner." He pulled out a chair for her. "That bank closing does have a good side to it, you know," he said as he carried their coffee to the table and set out forks, a knife, two small plates, and the pie tin.

"What could possibly be good about it, Andrew? That makes no sense." Eva scowled and placed a piece of pie on one of the plates, pushing it across the table toward him.

"Because they *are* closed. I don't know for sure what that means, but I bet it's going to buy me some time before they try to repossess any of my equipment. Time is always good. And there's another reason: me and you." He set his cup down and took her hand again. "Eva, we ain't going to do this. I just realized we're turning into my parents. They loved each other to death, but they never talked, never knew what the other one was thinking, or wanted, or how they felt. We ain't going to be like that, you hear me? No more secrets. No more pride. No more lies or half-truths. Okay?"

Eva nodded and swallowed hard. Andrew said nothing more, only turned and went into their room and shut the door.

Even though most people in Wayland didn't have much—or any—money in the bank in Fort Blackmore, most of them were almost as nervous and frantic and numb as Eva. They knew something bad was happening, that more bad was going to happen, and they huddled together, frozen in place as they waited for whatever was coming.

Down at Blair's Store, more men than usual gathered to drink coffee and talk, leaving their work idle in the fields and barns. They hoped someone would come by with news that the bank had opened back up, or that the state or federal government had a plan, and everything was going to be all right. But the news didn't look good.

Rumors flew fast and furious, saying several sawmills and one of the county's grain mills would be shut down until further notice. One man said a prominent family in the area, the McConnells, had lost a huge sum of money in the bank, and that old man McConnell had become so distraught, they had to get neighbors to come and remove all the guns from his house for fear he would do himself harm. The McConnells were some of the biggest tobacco farmers in that side of the county, and if they lacked money to operate, there would be a lot of people without spending money for the year.

Andrew did not join the crowds of idle workers. He went on to the mill and stayed busy. He had a big job to finish up, and as far as he knew, the people who were going to pay him had their money in Gate City bank, and there was no reason to think he wouldn't get paid. But if the Fort Blackmore bank went under, they might all go. He wanted to withdraw his money as fast as he could. The big question was where the next job would come from. People would be scared of their own shadows now, even the ones who hadn't lost money. Andrew's eyes filled with tears to think he might lose everything, that Eva might wind up right back where she started when they married—with practically nothing.

✦

While the world was crumbling for Andrew and lots of his neighbors, as well as people all across the country, Buddy Newman's ship had finally come in.

When Buddy Newman walked through the door of the town Mission, as he now did almost every other day, he immediately strode to the front desk where Molly gave out supplies. Her hair was wet with perspiration, and without waiting for him to ask, she said, "No, nothing for you, Buddy."

Buddy looked around at the room full of the world's lost, desperate souls with their gaunt faces and bleeding feet, the most hobos he'd ever seen come off the train at the same time. Things were definitely not getting any better. *It's time for me to move on.*

"Are you sure, dear? I'm expecting something very important." Buddy gave her his sweetest smile.

"Oh, OK. I'll check again." Molly rose from her chair with a groan and walked toward the mail pile.

Buddy followed behind her and saw the envelope addressed to him at the top of the stack. "That's it! That's it." He grabbed the letter from her hand, trying to cover the return address.

"You in trouble, Buddy?" She frowned at him.

"Oh no, sweet lady. Quite the opposite." Buddy smiled down at the attorney's return address and then stuck the letter in his inside coat pocket. "As Mr. Tennyson has said, 'And wheresoe'er thou move, good luck / Shall fling her old shoe after.' I bid you a good day, good madam." Buddy turned on his heel and strutted out of the place, grinning ear to ear.

Only when he got far out of town, far into some brush and trees at the edge of town and he was satisfied no one would see, did he take the envelope out of his pocket and open it. It was a note from the attorney who had taken care of his father's property, telling him the farm sold for $1,882 and, after the lawyer took his fee, he had deposited the remainder of $1,782.34 in a bank account in Bluefield, which amount could be retrieved anytime upon request. Buddy slapped his leg and hollered, "Whoo-ee!" No more begging and starving and stinking for him. No more putting up with lowlife sons-of-bitches like Iron Mike. He'd go get that money and get him a roof over his head and a new suit of clothes and new shoes.

Besides, Buddy knew his time in Wayland was coming to a close. He could see a difference now in the way people reacted to him. No more back slapping and smiles. He blamed it on Mac or Eva, or both. They must be talking him down. Most people were back to looking at him as just another hobo, not to be trusted, much less be friendly with—the lowest sort of man.

The money had arrived at the perfect time. He could do what he'd been dreaming of for months and then find a dream place to live. A city somewhere, a place he might sell his art on the street, do portraits of pretty women and girls. It was going to be a great life, the one he deserved. There was only one more thing he wanted to do first, one last little reward he wanted for himself. He chuckled as he thought of Marvell's poem to the woman he lusted after:

> Now therefore, while the youthful hue
> Sits on thy skin like morning dew,
> And while thy willing Soul transpires
> At every pore with instant Fires,
> Now let us sport us while we may...

After talking about their mutual secrets, Eva felt uneasy with Andrew. She believed they both felt guilty for their dishonesty and embarrassed by their pride. They were extra polite with each other, nervous and hesitant, insecure. It was like their courtship all over again.

Eva felt nauseated all the time from the guilt she carried. She and Andrew had made a pact to have a true marriage with no secrets, no lies, no deceptions. Yet Eva could not bring herself to mention Buddy and the drawing again. She had talked herself out of it once more. The threat of losing everything now pressed harder on her heart than concerns about Buddy.

They still did the work that needed doing, fulfilling the silent agreement husbands and wives often have about how things get done. Andrew did the hard work of gathering and harvesting everything; Eva's job was to grow seedlings and save seeds, help plant, and then do all the canning and drying. He surprised her the evening he asked her to put on some old clothes and boots and come help dig potatoes, but it pleased her, too. He wanted her near, and that was a good sign.

They worked in silence mostly, Andrew using a little single plow to run down the rows and turn the potatoes out onto the ground like puzzle pieces. They rolled, sometimes half a dozen at a time, toward Eva's feet, and she scurried to gather them inside big grain sacks she'd saved.

By the time they finished, both their faces were flushed and pink, shiny with sweat, clothes wet from exertion. Andrew shed his wet shirt on the grass, and Eva grinned at him.

"Wish I could do that."

"I wish you could, too." He grinned back, raising his eyebrows, and Eva laughed out loud. It had been a long, long time since he'd flirted with her.

The cool evening air had finally stirred, the little breeze so welcome that Eva closed her eyes and held her arms out from her sides to draw it all in. The tree frogs began to sing, and Eva opened her eyes to a perfect gloaming, the sky a striped scarf of yellow, purple, blue, and pink that shifted and changed almost by the second. What a gift to end the day. Eva stood transfixed. She felt Andrew's eyes on her and grinned again. He took the last sack from her hands and dragged it over inside the fenced yard, along with the others.

"We'll dump them all out here to dry until tomorrow. We'll knock the dirt off of them and sack 'em back up then. We don't want to put those in the cellar wet, or they'll rot on us."

Eva didn't let him see her smile as she laughed to herself at his stating the obvious.

He sat down on the edge of the porch, and Eva sat beside him to admire the pile of good meals spread out before them. She studied his strong brown arm next to her skinny pale one, and she reached over and rubbed that bare skin. He flinched, and she heard his breath catch. When she put her other arm around his bare back, letting her fingertips brush across his neck, he turned and pulled her to his chest.

"Eva... Eva... I... I want to make you happy. And I..."

She stopped him with her fingers on his lips. "Andrew, you do. You have. 'Where you go I will go and where you lodge, I will lodge.' I remember Momma quoting that. We've just got to trust and leap when our heart tells us to, Andrew."

He cradled her head in one hand, rubbing a thumb along her check, and pulled her into a long, hard kiss. She felt his heart beating strong and fast against hers.

When the kiss finally ended, they went inside and called goodnight to Katie, who was reading in her room. They went to bed and made love as quietly as anyone could, but with such intensity that Eva thought her heart would burst. Afterward, they held each other and Eva cried, and they whispered for a long time. By the early hours of morning, they'd made the toughest decision of their lives.

Andrew had a friend who'd started working for the new chemical manufacturing plant being built just across the state line in Tennessee. A man named George Eastman had started manufacturing chemicals used in photography, and Kingsport was a bustling, busy place with hundreds of people showing up and landing jobs with the construction crews building the facility. Andrew's friend had told him there was need for a lot of sawed lumber, both rough and finished, and that his expertise and equipment could be put to good use. Andrew decided to pack an overnight bag and go over there to talk to someone in person.

If he could pull this off, he could sell his equipment to them and sell himself—as someone with the kind of skills they'd need. Then he, Eva, and Katie could move to Kingsport, be out of debt and have a paycheck coming in, letting someone else be responsible for making payroll and bank payments. The thought made Andrew feel as though a boulder had been lifted from his back, and he slept sounder than he had in months. He believed Eva slept like a baby, too, her back to Andrew's chest. The rhythm of her breath soothed him to sleep as he realized this new plan would also solve their other big problem: Buddy Newman.

33

Commandment

I have always puzzled over one of the commandments. The others—telling you not to lie, steal, kill, envy—have always made sense, even when I was a little kid. The fifth one, though, is just the opposite: I thought I understood it when I was a kid, but as an adult was completely puzzled by it. "Honor thy father and thy mother." It seems obvious when you're young. You have all kinds of ideas and impulses to do bad things when you are a kid, before you learn better. If you don't listen to your parents, you're liable to get in a lot of trouble and do things you'll regret.

After I became a grown woman, though, I wondered, surely all the commandments are for all of us for our whole lives. What grown person doesn't honor and respect their parents? Why would God go to the trouble of carving that in a stone tablet? Who doesn't learn by the time they are grown that your parents love you more than anyone and would never steer you wrong?

As I begin to see little signs of Katie rebelling, seeming to even be a bit resentful and angry, I started to think about this commandment. I thought about quoting it to her the other day, but I didn't, because the thought stopped me in my tracks—I am not her mother. What if Katie goes on the wrong track, all because I'm not her real mother?

I felt sick all day and did not sleep well that night at all. Because this is a fact: every person I've ever known who didn't respect and honor their parents, if they were hostile, resentful, disobedient and disrespectful, if they looked down their nose at their parents—they have sad lives. You never reach your full potential unless you not only love, but honor and respect them and their sacrifices, understand them and their values, admire them in some way.

To try to cast off your parents is to cast off the best part of your real self, and there is no way you can come to a good life that way. I pray that Katie comes out the other side of her teen years having made peace with her daddy, with me, with Andrew, and with her best self.

A Sign

I haven't been writing in here, Journal, because I just can't face myself and all that's going on here on this scary, blank page. I've got so many thoughts swirling that I can barely function. I worry about the bank awhile, then Katie, then Buddy, then what Edith said about Nancy and Buddy, about the drawing, back to the mill and our home. It's a sick, awful circle I'm trapped in.

I've prayed and prayed, read my Bible. I want some good news. I keep hoping God will send me a miracle, that somebody will ride by and say, "Oh, everything's OK. The bank is back open." It's not happened so far. Instead, people are all worried sick and hunkered down. They don't hardly come out of their houses except to go to church. And I want Buddy Newman to go crawl back into whatever miserable hole he crawled out of. I don't want to ever have to think about him again.

I did have something happen that gave me hope, though. I saw ball lightning the other night. I was walking over from the sawmill where I'd took Drew a tenderloin biscuit, and a storm blew up out of nowhere. The beautiful blue sky filled with huge white clouds that looked like lambs turned iron gray, and a wind blew from the north. Then all at once there was an explosion that nearly made me jump out of my skin, and I saw a ball of lightning roll right down God's arm, so to speak, and hit a big broken cherry tree across the back pasture. That tree exploded into pieces. That big ball was spinning and hissing, shooting little arcs of fire as it tumbled. When it hit the tree, the sound was loud as a cannon. It was one of the most amazing things I ever saw. I think it was some kind of sign. The trouble is that God often sends us signs, but they're in a language we don't understand.

Ruth

I stare at this white page and try to form the words right to name what I'm feeling—to be able to explain myself to myself, as crazy as that sounds. I realized this week that my neck and shoulders are staying tight as a banjo hide, tense and fearful all the way into the muscle and bone. I think I've figured out that it's because I have no confidence. I feel like I want to crawl back into bed, like I did after my baby died, just give up because the world is too much for me. Nothing ever works out for me. It's easy to give up on yourself and everything when you keep getting kicked down.

But then I remember my momma talking about Ruth. In the Bible, there are only a few women who get their stories told and held up as examples, and Ruth is one of them. After she loses everything, people expect her to give up but she doesn't. She goes to a whole new country of people who don't believe like she does. And she finds God and a husband and new land to love, and children.

Most of all, I suspect she found herself—her true unafraid self. Ruth didn't just find a husband, she found a man of true heart and integrity, and together they faced the world, no matter what obstacles the world put up, and there were many! I have had a similar experience, and I need to remember that.

34

Buddy headed back out to Wayland the next morning, cutting through woods and across Copper Creek, unable to believe his good fortune, how everything was falling into place for him. With his money safely tucked away. Buddy now had a clear path to achieve his long-delayed dream. Andrew had told him and Mac that he was going to be gone for a couple of days to "see about a big job," so the stars had aligned for Buddy's move.

After he finished with Katie, he could just pick up his knapsack full of money and head on out to his new life. And he had made a big decision that gave him a good feeling. Buddy had decided he would not take Katie's life.

With the money, he could move far away. He could go back to using his real name. Nobody would ever know where to look for a Buddy Newman who didn't exist. He would go back to shaving his head, too, and wearing nice clothes. No one would ever mistake him for some wandering bum. If they ever did come and find and accuse him, he'd just say it was crazy, and there'd be no way to prove it. He might live by the ocean—something he'd never seen. It would be a place to paint and draw, pick up odd jobs, and best of all, watch all the pretty women. He could imagine himself setting up a little stand somewhere on the beach where he'd offer to do quick drawings of the ladies and little girls for a modest sum. It would be a heavenly life.

Buddy knew Katie would probably be out with her friends since it was Saturday. He hoped so anyway—that would make his day much easier. If she was at home reading or doing chores, he'd have to come up with some way to lure her out of Eva's sight and not raise any alarm. He decided to check all the kids' haunts first. He went over to Copper Creek to their swimming hole, but no one was there. The next most likely spot was Alice's place. He just happened to remember the tree house and swung by there. Probably a long shot.

To his delight, he heard a little rustle and a voice as soon as the tree-house came into sight, and Katie popped her head out the window. She smiled and waved when she saw him.

"Hey, Buddy! What are you doing here?"

"Why, I'm looking for you, sweetheart. Are you up there by yourself?"

"Yes. Alice is coming when she finishes her chores. But why are you looking for me?"

"Well, I hadn't seen you for a day or two, and I missed you." He smiled at her, eager to try out the clever story he'd crafted as he approached the treehouse. "Crazy like, I left my fishing pole over on the creek. I got to watching a gang of turkeys and their babies, and I just got up and walked out of there without my pole. I reckon I'm going crazy. I thought you might like to walk over there with me and get it."

Katie shrugged. "Sure, I'll be right down."

They started off across the fields, Katie stopping to pick wildflowers from the field and pulling the petals off, telling Buddy about a book she was reading about John Audubon.

"He was the man who identified and drew a picture of every kind of bird in the country. Do you know about him? He was a great artist, like you."

Buddy began to tell her all about him, about seeing some of his work in a museum once, and Katie looked rapt, as always, and in awe of Buddy's knowledge and his life experiences. Buddy was having difficulty concentrating on what he was saying, his mind flashing little hot sparks of scenes of what he was about to do with Katie. His heart pounded and his body flushed with heat, little beads of perspiration forming on his brow and the back of his neck.

To his great disappointment, when he topped the ridge overlooking the creek, he saw a couple of fishermen below and knew he'd have to come up with an alternative plan. He'd have no privacy here. He needed time to play out his scene, though. He smiled to himself when he noticed a tree of his favorite kind of apple—spotted Smokehouse apples. He would come back to pick one after he finished. *I'll have a bite of the Tree of Good and Evil today.*

He took Katie's hand, and they walked on down to talk to the men, asking if they had seen a fishing pole. Buddy pretended to be very sad and disappointed when they said they hadn't, complaining about how it was all his own fault, but people were sorry and no count these days. Katie squeezed his hand and patted it with her other one.

"I'm sorry, Buddy. I bet Uncle Drew has an extra one you could borrow."

She looked up at him so sympathetically with those beautiful, deep eyes, and Buddy thought he would melt and flow away with the water trickling down the ridge toward Copper Creek.

Buddy suddenly had an idea, and it was all he could do not to laugh and jump up and down.

"You know what? I think there's one at the sawmill, now that you mention it, in that little storage shed. I know your uncle is gone and we can't ask him, but he wouldn't mind me using it. Let's go get it. What do you say?"

"Sure! Alice will know that if I'm not at the treehouse, I'm at the creek. She'll come find us once we're back."

35

Fresh from what he felt was a new start to his marriage, Andrew had set off with a smile and a little knapsack of clothes, a notebook with a list of all his equipment and how much he owed, and several biscuits. He'd ride his horse to Gate City where a friend in the courthouse would find someone with a car and the day off. That someone would take Andrew to Kingsport, where he'd see another man about buying his equipment. Andrew was so excited, he felt short of breath. This plan could work. Maybe it was all part of a bigger plan. Bad things sometimes forced people to change in ways that were much better in the long run.

Eva had given him a kiss and held his face in her hands. "Whatever happens, Drew, we're going to be fine. Don't fret. And don't linger, neither. Get on back here, soon as you can."

Eva watched Andrew until he was out of sight and then went back in and started working on her quilt. Nothing calmed her nerves like doing something with her hands. She looked forward to a day with just her and Katie, without Buddy and Andrew to deal with. Eva made Katie's favorite dish, fried pork loin and potatoes, and set the table. But noon came and went with no Katie. Eva paced the floor like a hound about to have pups.

The clock chimed one o'clock, and Eva suddenly felt a flash of alarm run down her back, a thunderhead building behind her eyes. She went ahead and started eating, but her hands were shaking and wouldn't stop. Katie was dependable, and she never missed a meal. Eva finally pushed her half-eaten dinner away. She quickly covered both plates with a clean towel and left the house, walking and running all the way to Alice's house. Along the way, she tried to reassure herself that Katie would be there having dinner with them or off playing in the creek, forgetful of the time of day. But when Alice appeared at the door with a puzzled look on her face and said she hadn't seen Katie, Eva turned with only a muttered goodbye and took off at a run again, back down the road. Mary and Henry didn't like company and wouldn't come to the door, people said. They'd come this time, or she'd kick the door in. *I pray that's where she is. Please, Lord, let her be there.*

Fearful of startling the old couple, Eva stood in the road and called out, "Mary! Mary? Can I talk to you please?" Hearing no response or movement from the house, she cautiously opened the front gate and stepped into the yard. The rickety wooden steps and porch floor barked under her anxious heels, and she winced at the sharp noise. She knocked softly and waited, hearing a faint rustle inside the house. Finally, the doorknob turned slowly and a wrinkled face peeked out a tiny crack in the door.

"Mary, you may not remember me..." she began, but Mary spoke in her hoarse voice.

"I know ye. You're that little girl's mother, Ezra Teague's sister."

"Yes, yes, I am. Mary, I'm looking for Katie. I know she's come over to visit you some. Have you seen her? I'm worried sick. It ain't like her to miss a meal."

Mary's eye widened, and she opened the door farther. She stood in a stained, ragged dress and a sweater with frayed cuffs. Her hair stuck out all around her head in wiry gray spikes. "I bet I can find her. We'll go look."

Mary led her around behind the house and over the hill, back up through a neighbor's pasture and across another one to the creek. Eva was exhausted and thirsty, but she kept up, marveling at what good shape Mary was in for an old woman. "Where are we going?" Eva pushed a sapling limb out of her face with both hands as they raced through the timber.

"The swimmin' hole," Mary said over her shoulder. "Them young'uns go there all the time." But at the crest of the hill, Mary stopped and set her mouth in a straight line. Eva was still huffing and puffing up the hill behind her when Mary turned and shook her head. "Ain't here," Mary said. "I got one more idea."

Eva was more anxious than ever. How did Mary know so much about what the kids did? It didn't make sense. Everybody said she never left the house, was just a crazy hermit. When Eva realized Mary was leading her back over the hill away from both their homes, toward Andrew's sawmill, she stopped and put her hands on her knees to rest a minute and catch her breath. "Stop, Mary. Stop."

Mary obliged and turned to stare at her with a blank look.

"Why would she be at the sawmill? That is where you're going, right?"

"Cause that's where he mighta took her." Mary reached in her pocket and pulled out a little square of tobacco and a pocket knife, sliced off a piece, and tucked it inside her jaw.

Eva's dinner rose into her throat, and she let out a little cry and a moan all at once. She *knew*, but still she hoped she was wrong. "Who are you talking about? He, who?"

"That drifter." Mary folded the knife and stuck it back in her apron. "He's not good. He follows them young'uns all the time. I seen him."

For the second time, Buddy Newman made Eva's heart stop in its tracks, made her mind shift to another reality, screaming and crying, taking her to her knees on the ground—but it was all just imagined. At that moment, she saw as clear as the hawk circling above did. She broke into a run, sprinting past Mary and toward the mill as fast as her legs would carry her, toward the danger she now knew was very real

Eva was in a sweat by the time she reached the mill, her hair in damp ringlets sticking to her face and neck, the collar of her dress soaked. She'd run most of the way to the little shed where Buddy kept his things. There in his knapsack, she found his drawings, including the one of Katie. But the sketch was not what now chilled her blood, made her teeth chatter, in spite of the heat and exhaustion. This time she found a few newspaper clippings in there—a death announcement of some people up in Russell County and a yellowed article, an account of a murder.

In September of 1929, a squirrel hunter had found the nude body of thirteen-year-old Polly Baker in a wooded area in the northern part of Tazewell County, Virginia. Because her only family was her grandmother who had raised her, and because Polly was a willful and rowdy child, the article said, everyone thought she had run away. She'd been found in the woods, spread out, arms and legs wide, with a little halo of stones placed around her head. A symbol had been carved into her arm and an apple wedged inside her mouth as though she were a pig about to be roasted.

The clipping, thin as a locust wing, fluttered in her trembling hands. *Why would he be carrying this? Was the girl a relative or neighbor?* A possible answer came into her mind, but she couldn't bear to think it, would not give words to the horrible realization that was forming. Eva barely made it out of the shed before throwing up all her food, sobbing on her knees. Terror like she'd never felt before roiled in her wrung-out stomach, along with guilt and disbelief. She had no idea what to do next, where to look. She was sweating and chilling at the same time, unable to pull herself to her feet.

Mary stood over Eva, her mouth set in a grim line. "You go on back home. There's always a chance she'll come home. I'm going to go send somebody for the sheriff."

36

Andrew burst into the house not long after Eva returned. He grinned and immediately launched into his tale of success and hopefulness, sure it would send Eva rushing into his arms, flashing that big freckled smile that still melted his heart. He talked a mile a minute, quoting the dollar figure that had been mentioned as a price for his equipment, the sizeable wages that sounded like a small fortune to him. He stopped, puzzled by Eva's frazzled, dazed appearance, her lack of a reaction.

"Honey, what's going on?" He sat down slowly in the kitchen chair.

"There's something else I have to tell you. It's about Buddy. I think..." Eva stopped for a minute and swallowed hard. Her words came out in a whisper. "Something bad has happened. Katie is... I don't know where she is. And I don't know what to do."

For a moment, Andrew's head spun; he imagined that the walls of the kitchen moved in closer to him and then back out again.

"I know you love Buddy like a brother, Drew, and I've put off telling you because of that, and because I thought you might not believe me. But I've got to try to get you to see: he ain't who you think he is. Buddy is not a good man. He's twisted."

Andrew's breathing came harder as Eva told him, fumbling for words, that she'd found a lewd drawing of their little girl in Buddy's backpack. She laid the drawing in front of him first, and then the article. He peered at her intently and felt the blood rush to his face. All of a sudden, it was as if he'd woken, wild-eyed, from a dream. It was all as clear as a July sky to him now. He jumped up from the chair and started out the door.

"Eva! What in the world..." He turned around toward her, then started back out again, and then turned to face her again. "Why in the world would you not tell me something like that? Whining to me about him not liking your cooking and silly stuff like that, when all along you knew this! I can't believe it."

Eva collapsed into a ball on the floor, sobbing now. Andrew bent down to her like she was a sleeping baby and pulled her up to his chest.

"No, I can't... It's not you to blame. I'm sorry, Eva. Shh. Stop now."
Eva tried to apologize, to explain her fear.

"No." Andrew stood up now and pulled her to her feet. "We'll talk about all of this later, Eva. Like I said, we're not doing this. No more. No more." He grabbed his rifle from behind the kitchen door. "You stay here in case she comes home or... if someone was to find her hurt or sick somewhere, they'd bring her here."

"Andrew! What are you going to do? Andrew!" Eva called after him as he strode off across the back field. "You aren't going alone!"

"No, no." He stopped and looked over his shoulder. "I've got a friend who can help me. A true friend. You stay here in case Katie comes home. Me and Mac will go look for her." He shook his head. "And we'll take care of Buddy."

Andrew put his horse into a run toward Mac's property. When he came flying up to the house, hollering Mac's name, Mac's wife opened the door. She looked puzzled and confused to see Andrew outside her door, still on his horse.

"He ain't here." She spoke before Andrew had time to ask. "I figured he was with you. Said he had to work on a problem at the mill, a part that tore up or something. Is everything... are you all right?"

"I need his help, is all. I'll go find him. Thanks." And with that, Andrew urged his horse into a full gallop down the dirt road toward the mill. As he rounded a curve, there stood Mary Johnson at the edge of the road in front of her house. She raised one hand in greeting, and he brought the horse to a stop beside her, the dry dust covering them all in a cloud.

"Have you seen my daughter? I'm looking for her." He caught himself and paused. He rarely called Katie that; he usually said "our girl" or even "Eva's niece."

"Like I told your wife, I suspect he's got her—that drifter. He follows them young'uns all the time." Mary spit a little amber star of tobacco into the dust at her feet. "I seen that other man that works for ye, that Mac fellow. He come by here just a while ago, too. But that drifter, he'll take her someplace where they ain't no people, where he feels comfortable."

Andrew had never before heard Mary string that many words together and certainly never dreamed she would know all of these things that he didn't know, all happening right under his nose.

"I was just fixin' to find somebody to go get the sheriff. Do you want me to do that, or do you want to fix this on your own?"

Mary set her mouth in a tight line and stared into Andrew's face. He understood what she was asking him. If, God forbid, Buddy had hurt Katie, it was better for them to handle it themselves. *Nobody has to know, and the world will be better off.* Andrew relaxed his clenched jaws at the thought, and at that moment, he became a soldier again. Buddy was now an enemy, like the Germans, just as if he'd been a soldier on the battlefield.

"Thanks. I'll take care of it." Andrew rode off again, leaving Mary standing in the swirling dust, her hands clasped together as if in prayer.

37

When Mac started back to the mill to repair a gear on one of the saws, his mind was a million miles away thinking of spring planting, worrying where their next big mill job would come from, reminding himself to check on his aging mother.

As he started to come out of the woods and into the clearing of the sawmill, he heard something. With Andrew gone, he'd closed down for the day and told the other men to enjoy some time at home. There shouldn't be anyone nearby. He froze in his tracks, thinking he was about to see a gang of thieves and wondering what in the world he'd do if they saw him and confronted him.

Nothing could have shocked him more than what he did see. For all his dislike and distrust of Buddy, he couldn't imagine him doing something this crazy. But there he was, leading Katie out of the woods by the hand, heading toward the little shed where he slept. Buddy was talking to Katie, soft and low and soothing, but Mac couldn't hear what he said. Mac stayed still as a doe in hunting season and watched Buddy lead her into the shed.

Once inside the shed, Buddy stayed in control and calm, though his heart was racing. He laid out his pad and pencils. Then he handed Katie an apple from his knapsack and told her to take off everything but her slip. Katie frowned, and a small puff of air, a half-laugh, escaped those rosebud lips.

"I don't know…" she said, giggling nervously.

"I forgot to tell you. I promised your Auntie I'd do a really nice drawing of you, like something in one of them big museums. You've heard of the Mona Lisa, ain't you?"

Katie nodded.

"Well, you're way prettier than her. I'm going to make you famous and everlasting. You'll see.

"I need you to show that pretty neck and shoulders of yours so I can do you justice. It's all right. I told Aunt Eva about all this, and she said it would be okay." Buddy's eyes widened and his breathing quickened. His heart pounded louder in his ears, and he saw something flash in Katie's eyes. Maybe doubt, definitely unease. He'd have to act fast. "I been wanting to draw you, Katie girl. Do a really good drawing of you, you know, something your Auntie and Andy can keep forever. You're just about the prettiest little girl I ever saw."

Mac moved soundlessly along the back of the mill, skirted the woods, and came up behind the shed. He could hear Buddy's voice through the thin walls, saying something about drawing Katie, saying she was the prettiest girl he'd ever seen.

Then Mac heard faint mumbling and shuffling, but he was afraid to move too much for fear of being discovered. He didn't know what Buddy would do if he caught Mac listening outside the shed, but he knew this all didn't feel right. Mac's pulse suddenly began racing, and he felt sick. Buddy wasn't just a troublemaker or a problem; he was much worse. Mac understood then that he might have to take Buddy's life. And that if it became necessary, he would.

Mac crept around to the front of the shed. He stood to one side and spotted Katie through the small window in the office door. Her eyes were wide and frightened, like those of a little calf in a chute.

Mac risked inching closer to take a better look. Buddy spoke softly again, although Mac couldn't understand his words. But Katie's voice rose sharply, and Mac heard panic and tears in her words: "I want to go *now* and find Alice!"

Mac stuck his head out a little farther to try to spot exactly where Buddy was. He had only a split-second view before Katie saw him. Mac put his fingers to his lips. Buddy had Katie, wearing only her slip, posed on a little stack of wooden boxes, her head tilted back, pretending to take a bite of a big red apple. Her other arm curved upward, her free hand smoothing her hair.

Despite the signal, Mac saw Katie glance at the door a second time, and Buddy must have seen it, too. He whirled around just as Mac stormed inside, hitting Buddy squarely in the nose, blood flying in all directions.

Katie dropped the apple and backed up against the wall of the shed. She looked puzzled, relieved, and terrified all at the same time. Stunned for a moment, Buddy smeared the blood with the back of his hand, but it was his other hand that brought a scream from Katie as Buddy pulled out a knife from his boot. As he started to lunge toward Mac, the sound of hooves came from the log yard, and they both hesitated. Mac called out, "He's got a knife, Andrew!"

Andrew burst through the door, his rifle leveled at Buddy's chest. Buddy didn't move, his face a mask of indecision mixed with fury. Katie skirted the wall as far from Buddy as possible, her lips trembling. "Uncle Drew!" Katie sobbed, clutching him around the waist. Andrew's face had turned white as a sheet.

"Did he hurt you, Katie?" Andrew handed the rifle to Mac and knelt down in front of her. "You can tell me, honey."

"No, no, he just acted strange. He made me hold an apple in my mouth while he drew me."

She broke into sobs once more, and Andrew just held her, patting her lightly. He looked helplessly at Mac, repeating again and again, "Shh, shh, it's all over."

38

Even as it was all happening, Andrew couldn't believe it. Buddy looked shocked and enraged. He glared at Mac with such hatred that it unnerved Andrew, but Mac never let the gun barrel drop from eye level. He told Andrew he'd hold the rifle on Buddy while Andrew took Katie home.

When he arrived home, Eva ran out of the house, and Katie headed straight into her arms, starting to cry again.

"She's all right, Eva. He didn't hurt her. Mac got there before I did." Andrew hugged them both as Eva also began to cry and stroke Katie's hair. "I'll be back soon. Don't worry." He kissed Eva's forehead and brought her and Katie inside. After giving Katie another awkward hug, Andrew grabbed his daddy's old pistol. He ran out into the evening air and hitched up the team and wagon. He didn't have much daylight left to do what needed to be done.

When Andrew returned to the shed, he and Mac marched Buddy outside and made him climb up onto the wagon. Andrew bound him with a big thick rope used to work cattle. They wrapped it a dozen times around his ankles and then tied it to the front of the wagon frame. If he did jump out of the wagon, he'd have had no way to free himself. He'd have had to lie there until morning, but, of course, Andrew was taking no chance on that.

"If he starts moving, if he throws himself out of the wagon," he stopped and looked at Buddy long and hard, without blinking, "shoot him. We'll untie him and leave him there. Let the sheriff think somebody, like somebody's jealous husband or one of these women he's used, finally rid the world of him. I'd prefer not to do it that way, but I will if I have to."

Buddy's face had turned pale. "So what do you aim to do with me, after treating me like no more than an animal?"

"I mean to put you on a train heading out of here, that's what. I want you as far away as I can get you. And understand this, Buddy, if I ever see you around these parts, I'll find a way, somehow, to get rid of you once and for all. I'll shoot you on sight and make it look like I caught you robbing me." Andrew stared Buddy in the eye, hatred heating his face.

Buddy lay back against the side of the wagon, looking sullen and dejected. Only a faint glow came from the half moon and clear night sky above. When they passed from under a canopy of trees blocking that little bit of light, Andrew felt a chill, as though they were passing a mountain stream, but it was only moonlight revealing the pure evil of Buddy, who glared at Andrew with narrowed eyes.

At the train station, they found a place to park just off the road behind some trees and overgrowth. Andrew took the heavy roping off Buddy's legs and the shotgun from Mac. He marched Buddy to the last open car of the train and made him climb inside. Andrew held the gun on him and gave Mac time to also climb up into the car. Mac again held the gun on Buddy while Andrew pulled himself into the car and tied Buddy's wrists and ankles once more.

"You might ought to rethink it, Andrew." Mac spit his tobacco juice on the ground without ever taking his eyes off his friend. "You'll always be looking over your shoulder."

"Ha, ha!" Buddy sneered. "You better believe it, Andrew. Just over your shoulder."

Andrew whirled around and stuck his pistol against Buddy's jawbone, pulling back the hammer.

"Oh, I don't think so, Mac. He knows I've been trained to deal with killing somebody who needs killing, right, Buddy?" Andrew shoved the pistol butt hard against Buddy's face, making him wince. Even when Buddy tried to turn his head and pull away, Andrew gritted his teeth and shoved the pistol butt harder into his cheekbone. "Right, Buddy?"

Andrew reached into his coat pocket and brought out two large bandanas that he tied together to make a gag. He knotted the cloth firmly over Buddy's open mouth. Andrew watched until he was sure no one could see them, and then he and Mac jumped clear of the car. They hid in the laurel thicket along the track, watching until the crew finished refueling and letting freight on and off. When the train finally pulled out of the station, Andrew felt lighter than he had in months. The nightmare was over, and life could go back to normal. Mac and Andrew watched the train until it rumbled out of sight.

"I don't know, Andrew." Mac shook his head and stared at the toe of his boot. "I don't know what we should have done. He might come right back here, just like a bad dream. Maybe we need to go get the sheriff."

"And tell him what, Mac? This hobo who's been practically living with us for months has been drawing dirty pictures, and then we caught him taking our girl inside the shed and drawing her. What will he be charged with?" Andrew stopped and paced for a minute. He rubbed his hands through his hair and put his hat back on. "No, we ain't got a thing on him, Mac. Everybody in the country would just be gossipin' from now on, that's all. It would ruin Eva—and Katie, too. No. I won't put them through that."

Andrew stared at his own boot tops. Mac had a point about the possibility of Buddy coming back, but he would deal with that if it happened. "He's a smart man. That's to our favor. If he shows up here again, surely he knows what that means: I'll have to trade my life for his."

Mac looked back toward the train station and nodded. "You're right. Nobody would do a thing."

The men said no more and headed back to the wagon, Andrew hoping they could ride it right back into the way the world used to be.

On the train, the heat was already rising in the boxcar, and so was Buddy's white-hot rage. The swaying motion of the train banged him around, making it difficult to work on freeing his hands from the ropes. The longer that took him, the longer it was going to take to get back to the Nettles' place and do what had to be done.

His backpack was still at the shed, and no way was he leaving without his money. Plus, he had unfinished business with that little girl. She had toyed and tempted him long enough, smiling up at him, bringing him coffee, asking him to teach her things and make her things. Women were all the same, just little harlots who wanted to make him crazy and then tell him "no." Just like his daddy had told him: women were the ruination of the world and the good men who ran it. Men had to have them to keep the human race going, but if it wasn't for that, there wouldn't be reason to keep none of them around except for pleasure. *If it wasn't for what they were sitting on, we ought to kill every one of them.*

When Buddy finally freed his limbs from the ropes and swung the car doors open to look for a place to jump, his mind was flashing images of

Katie naked, him on top of her, and he moaned a little as he often did when he had such thoughts. He saw Eva, too, screaming under him, as he bit into the warm melon of her shoulder, tasted the blood in his mind, and he gave one of his little grunts again. That little bitch would pay. When the train finally approached a place with a nice sloping green bank to catch his fall beside the track, he moved to break free of the car and fly to freedom, only maybe ten miles from the station, a fairly short walk back to the sawmill and the Nettles' home and the fulfillment of his long-held fantasies. When he pushed off the side of the door, he expected to fly and feel the thud of his feet hitting the ground, and then the shock vibrating up through him as he rolled onto his shoulders into a ball, as he'd done dozens and dozens of times. Instead, when he leapt, his ragged coat caught on the thick, rusty hinge of the railcar door, and he slammed hard against the side of the car, the tearing fabric the last sound he heard as he fell beneath the speeding train, landing at just the perfect position for the train to send his severed head tumbling down the embankment like a big green cabbage falling off a farm wagon.

39

The next day was unlike any Sunday afternoon the family had ever passed. Katie, Eva, and Andrew all stayed at home, uneasy and on edge. Every little sound brought one of them to the window. Andrew had stood his rifle in the corner by the front door, and the shotgun was near the back door in the kitchen. Both he and Eva had big dark circles under their eyes—they'd barely slept since Andrew and Mac put Buddy on that train.

"I hope it ain't always like this, Drew." Eva looked out across the pasture at the beloved, magic willow tree she so dreaded leaving behind. Andrew had told her he planned to accept the job offer in Kingsport. "Will we always be looking over our shoulder? Jumping at every sound?"

Eva knew Katie must have many questions she wanted to ask, but she seemed afraid to ask them. Katie even acted as though *she* had done something wrong. Eva would have a long talk with Katie once things settled down. It was time to help Katie understand what growing up and becoming a woman meant.

When they heard the sound of a horse outside, Eva flew to the window and peeped out between the curtains, her face lighting up like it was Christmas morning.

"It's Ezra! Katie, come see—it's your daddy! I can't believe it." Eva ran to the door and rushed out to greet him. Someone she didn't know had brought Ezra on a wagon pulled by a team of mules, and he smiled down at Andrew, Katie, and Eva. His wife and one of his older girls sat behind him in the second seat. Ezra's appearance shocked Eva. He was gaunt and pale, and she noticed immediately when he raised his hand and called "Hello!" that his hand looked strange.

Ezra's wife Mary Anne said, "Hello! We hope we haven't come at a bad time. He just took a notion, and there was no time to write you." She looked at Andrew and motioned for him to come closer. "You'll have to help him down and into the house." At that, she pulled two crutches from the floor of the wagon.

Eva watched for Katie's reaction, but she only stared and said nothing.

"Yes, I been meaning to write you all, but I just couldn't figure out how to spell it out. And then when I got Katie's letter, I knew I had to come in person."

Eva looked at Katie with a frown. "A letter? What letter?"

Katie dropped her eyes and twisted her hands together.

The man driving the wagon tied off the mules and then climbed back up on the wagon to help Ezra to his feet. Ezra looked at Mary Anne, then Eva, and then Katie, and he chuckled and blushed. Eva saw that Ezra couldn't completely straighten up, but stood with his legs slightly bent at the knees. The driver stooped over and picked Ezra up in his arms in a sitting position, the way a man might carry his bride over a threshold on their wedding night. Eva's mouth flew open, and it took her a minute to come to herself and close it. She tried to compose herself, realizing she must look horrified.

"If you'll help me set him on the ground, sir," the driver said to Andrew, "he can use his crutches to walk up to the porch, and then we can carry him in."

Ezra laughed nervously. "I wasn't worth the trouble to fool with when I was healthy, Andrew. I sure ain't worth the trouble now. There's a church over where we live that's going to get me one of them wheelchairs, and that will help a whole lot."

After finally getting Ezra inside the house and everyone settled down, coffee made and water poured and pleasantries passed around, the man who had brought Ezra and his family set down a satchel and a burlap bag that Eva could tell held Ezra's banjo. The driver looked at all of them with pity and tipped his hat as he left. An awkward silence fell over the room. Eva had already flashed a look at Andrew and Katie that said, *Not one word. He has enough burden without telling him any of this, at least for now.*

There was no way Eva was going to try to explain the events of the day before, of the months before, when they'd almost let a terrible man hurt Ezra's daughter. No way she was telling him they were about broke, that the bank lost all their money. Eva just couldn't bear the thought of adding anything else to Ezra's burden. She felt so sorry for him, and tears threatened to spill from her eyes.

It was obvious to her, though, that there was more to this visit than a brother dropping in on his sister. He hadn't been here in several years. And there was still the mention of the mysterious letter.

"What letter?" Eva asked again. "Can somebody tell me what's going on?"

Katie suddenly burst into tears and put her head down. Ezra made a terrible face, as if he, too, could barely contain his emotions. At that, Katie rose and put her arms around his neck and sobbed.

"Now, now, sweet girl." He patted her with a gnarled hand.

"I'm sorry. I... I shouldn't have sent that. I don't know what got into me."

Eva sighed in frustration, and Andrew looked puzzled as well as nervous. He continued to glance out through the curtains from time to time.

"I sent Daddy a letter, Aunt Eva, about how much I missed him, and told him I wished I had some small pictures of my momma."

"She just wanted to ask me questions, Eva. It's fine. She's growing up—not a little girl anymore." Ezra smiled sadly.

He held Katie's hand as she turned and sat down closer to him. "I swear, if you ain't the spittin' image of your momma, I don't know who is. I bet you're sweet and smart and strong like her, too. I come all the way over here so you could see me, see what a shape I got in, so you'd know why I ain't been to see you, and why I don't write like I used to. I can't."

Ezra glanced at Eva and Andrew and then looked back at Katie as he held up his twisted hands, the fingers pulled almost down to his palms, knuckles swollen and misshaped by arthritis. "My toes are doing the same thing."

"I'm so sorry. I didn't know, but I should have. I should have known there was a good reason." Katie wiped her eyes with her sleeve.

The letter had been a lashing out, Eva realized, a cry of hurt or loneliness or both. No matter that she and Andrew had loved Katie all they could, done all they could—nothing and no one could replace a mother and father. Eva couldn't help but wonder if Buddy hadn't been planting that idea in her head, too, that she needed a daddy. Of course, he would do that. The thought chilled Eva, and she just knew he was the motivation for the letter, playing off circumstances to his advantage.

"We ain't going to be sad no more." Ezra let go of Katie's hand and pointed toward his bags. "Bring me my banjo, girlie, and let's have a tune."

"Now Ezra," Mary Anne started to say, "you know that makes your hands hurt and..."

"Hush now, darling. A man ought to sing for his family if he's able at all. I might not get a chance again."

Katie handed him the banjo, though it was obvious he wasn't going to be able to play the way Eva remembered. But his thumb still worked a bit, and so he at least strummed a chord that sounded in tune, and he sang Katie a funny old song, "Froggy Went A-Courtin'," that made her laugh out loud. Eva laughed, too, and she couldn't stop the tears that leaked out with her laughter.

Even Andrew smiled and chuckled and seemed to forget about looking out the window or jumping at every sound.

"I hope it's all right if we stay tonight, Eva." Ezra had set his banjo down, and Katie shyly plucked at the strings as he talked. "I just can't imagine climbing back on that wagon again today, so I told the driver to come pick us up tomorrow. Next time I come, I promise I'll give you fair warning and not surprise you like this."

"Oh, don't be silly. I wouldn't care if you stayed a week. I'm happy to rest my eyes on you. I've missed you, too. And actually..." she stopped and looked at Drew. She knew he probably wasn't keen on the idea of revealing his plans just yet, but it felt right to her. Katie and Ezra needed to know what was coming.

"Actually, we're probably going to be moving. We'll be a lot closer to you, Ezra."

"What?" Katie's eyes grew as big as silver dollars. "Where are we going? Why?"

Eva didn't tell them everything. But she told them Andrew had a real opportunity with the new company in Kingsport, that he could sell his sawmill to them, go over there and run it for them, and have more money than he'd ever had in his life. "It's an opportunity we feel like we can't pass up, though we'll surely miss it here." Wistful, Eva looked around the house.

"We're going to be living in town, in Kingsport?" Katie's eyes were still wide, but a smile was starting to curl up her cheeks.

Ezra grinned from ear to ear. "Did you hear that, honey? I can't believe it." He beamed at his wife. "I was just going to tell you and Andrew that we're moving closer to Kingsport, too. Now that I can't work, Mary Anne's brother is going to let us stay in a little apartment in the back of his store over in Sullivan Gardens. He says we can keep an eye on things that way. They're going to start selling gasoline for cars, and he says me and her can keep up with the money and the record keeping, and he'll do everything else. He can't read too good."

Ezra took Katie's hand again. "You hear that, Sissy? We'll just about be neighbors. You can come see me." He winked and wiggled his eyebrows. "I'll let you have some free candy. My brother-in-law won't miss it."

"Why, Ezra, you're meaner than a striped snake!" Mary Anne said, and they all laughed. Eva felt a warm rush of relief, unable to believe that in the space of an hour or two, life could take such an unforeseen turn, that such happiness and hope could be building.

40

The next morning, as promised, the man showed up with the wagon to take Ezra back to Gate City. There he would hitch a ride with a business-man who made a little money on the side transporting people with his car. Andrew asked the driver to wait outside for a few minutes while Ezra and Mary Anne said their goodbyes.

This time when they all gave each other hugs, it felt different to Eva. They had a plan, and they had each other. Nothing could bring Alma back or give Ezra a body without disease or return Eva's money. Nothing could change the fact that they'd trusted the Devil himself and let him into their home. But there was a bond born of promise now, of time together, of reminiscing and laughing.

Ezra bent over and kissed the top of Katie's head. He reached into his pocket and pulled out a locket, handing it to her.

"I didn't give this to you yesterday because..." he stopped as the words and breath seemed to catch in his throat. "Because I couldn't handle it. But I got this for you. There's a photo of your mother inside. You need to not just carry her in your heart, invisible. You need to carry her outside it, too, where everybody can see her and remember her through you."

Katie opened the locket and found the tiny picture—her mother Alma on her wedding day. She held a little bouquet of irises, and her smile was joyous. It was true what they had said of her. She was incredibly beautiful.

The wagon hadn't been gone but an hour or so. Eva, Katie, and An-drew were cleaning and catching up with their chores. Andrew was still very much on edge, alert at every sound, looking out the windows every few minutes whenever he was inside the house. He needed to go to the mill, but he was scared, afraid Buddy hadn't believed him and was at the moment making his way back through the woods toward the house. Andrew sat in the rocker by the window and tried to stop thinking about it all, suddenly exhausted. He nodded off briefly but bolted straight out of his chair at the sound of someone walking up to the front porch. Eva and Katie stopped what they were doing and stared at the door. Andrew was already reaching for the rifle, but then he heard Mary's voice. He opened the door, and there she stood with Buddy Newman's familiar brown backpack.

"Mr. Nettles. This here belonged to that tramp. He left it in your shed. They's a lot of money in there." She handed it to Andrew.

"Money?" Eva's eyes were wide. "Where did he get a lot of money? Do you reckon that's why you're in trouble at the mill, Andrew? Was he stealing from you?"

Andrew shot Eva a dirty look and tightened his lips. He sure didn't want that news out in the community. Why give the gossips the satisfaction?

"No—no, ma'am. I read the letter that come with it." Mary shrugged. "If you're gonna take a man's backpack, it ain't gonna make it no worse to read what's in it. He got money from selling his momma's house and land. It's about eighteen hundred in there. Sounds like you all could use it. For all these months of feeding him and putting up with him. What a scare he's put you through! You deserve it. Don't think nothing about it."

She looked over at Katie and smiled a little. Her face grew serious then, and she stared at the floor. Andrew exchanged a look with Eva and thought of all the talk they'd heard over the years about Mary's state of mind.

Mary looked up at Andrew and Eva again. "I have to tell you something. I'm happy to do it, though it's a bad thing. My cousin come to see me yesterday and told me something. Said a man, a hobo from the looks of him, tried to jump off a train down about five or six miles from the Fort, and he fell. Said the train cut his head clean off. They had to go hunt for it in the bushes."

Eva gasped and then shook her head. "That coulda been anybody. Anybody!"

"No." Mary said emphatically. "No, ma'am. It was him. God told me." She reached into the backpack and pulled out a newspaper. "Here, read it for yourself. The article says he was probably a hobo, on account of his clothes and him being hid away in an empty car, but they didn't find any of his belongings or anything. They found part of his coat stuck in the door hinge."

Mary smiled at Katie again and stepped closer to her as she watched the expression on Katie's face change. Wide-eyed, Katie covered her mouth with her hands, as if to stop a scream.

Eva believed Katie still hadn't fully made sense of it all, that the kindly old man who treated her like a grandpa was not who she thought he was, that someone could be so different from who they appeared to be. She felt it would be a long time before Katie could trust a stranger again.

Mary patted Katie's back lightly. "When thou liest down, thou shalt not be afraid: yea, thou shalt lie down, and thy sleep shall be sweet. Be not afraid of sudden fear, neither of the desolation of the wicked, when it cometh. For the Lord shall be thy confidence, and shall keep thy foot from being taken." Mary studied Katie's face again, shaking her head with what appeared to be wonder. "Thank you, Katie, for visiting me."

She turned and looked from Eva to Andrew, then to Eva again, and then laughed a hearty laugh. "Go on," she said. "Go have a good life."

Mary let herself out, and Andrew reached for Eva's hand. He and Eva and Katie all watched from the doorway, Mary's voice becoming fainter as she sang a hymn and headed back down the dusty road to a man who thought she was an angel.

This will probably be my last entry for a good while. I sit here, amongst what looks like wreckage after a great storm, my life packed up in sacks and boxes, staring at the page, torn between two totally different frames of mind. One part of me is excited, hopeful, relieved. The other half is scared, nervous, exhausted. A body can't handle but so much stress and worry at once. My whole life and everything I thought would happen has been turned upside down. How could I have ever dreamed a year ago, feeling on top of the world, that such a change was coming?

Leaving this place is breaking my heart. I have loved this house, spent the best years of my life so far here. I love the trees in the yard and on the ridge, my flowers, my garden, the songbirds and this sky. To leave everyone I've known—my church, my family, those headstones in the cemetery—is so sad. And to know it will be just an occasional thing to come visit them all again—that is a hard adjustment.

I don't know what it will be like to live in town. I've never done it. But there will be good to it, I'm sure of it. My beautiful Katie will have so many new opportunities. She is excited to death! And she will be grown before we know it, with grandbabies to bring home to us. Imagine that! Andrew will make lots of new friends and love the challenge of building a factory. He has dreams of buying a Ford. He says I can help him do it by painting portraits of people's children and pets at Christmas. Now isn't he clever! And Katie wants to take music lessons. Everybody seems to have big plans.

It is what's best, for sure, and I trust Andrew absolutely on that. Who can question why things happen like they do? I don't know why this bank problem has come to wipe out all we've worked for, why Buddy Newman chose my house out of all the houses he could have stolen from, why the bank that had my money closed while others stayed in business. But here's what I do know: my momma is smiling and clapping her hands looking down on all this, and I can hear her voice plain as day saying, "See? Every time, God is faithful. Look how He sent you back double the money you lost." And she would laugh and shake her head again. Because she's right—there was about double the amount I lost at the bank in that knapsack Buddy left behind.

I've never been as solid as Momma was, never understood her patience in the face of such constant struggle and trial. But maybe I'll get there with time. If there's any rhyme or reason to any of this, it's the change it has brought in me and in Andrew and in us together. I don't think I'll ever go back to my old scared self, won't go back to my secrets and fears, and I will certainly never be the trusting soul I was, that's for sure. I now know that the devil looks just like us, and that some so-called "crazy people" like Mary are sometimes more in touch than anybody.

Most important, I do think we have to remember: there must still be a plan working for good somewhere. It's got us moving toward a better life, with me and Andrew more solid than ever. We may have tied the knot a long time ago, but we didn't double-knot it until all this happened. We'll never go back to our old ways of silence and secrets. It's a new day.

Rita Quillen's full-length poetry collection, *The Mad Farmer's Wife*, was published in 2016 by Texas Review Press (a Texas A&M affiliation) and was a finalist for the Weatherford Award in Appalachian Literature from Berea College. Her novel, *Hiding Ezra* (Little Creek Books), was a finalist for the 2005 DANA Awards. One of six semi-finalists for the 2012-14 Poet Laureate of Virginia, she has received three Pushcart nominations and a Best of the Net nomination in 2012.

For more information visit: www.ritasimsquillen.com.